"You're Going to Kill Us Both!"

Chris's eyes darted around the Ferris wheel car. He put his hands on the safety bar and began rocking.

"I'll tip this thing over," he threatened. "You're a tease, aren't you! Admit it, Tina!"

The car tilted forward.

"Chris," Tina cried. "Stop. We're going to fall out."

"Then kiss me," he insisted, moving closer. "Kiss me now!"

"No!" Tina shouted.

Chris used his weight to swing the car.

Back and forth. Back and forth.

"Chris! Are you crazy?" Tina shrieked.

Books by R. L. Stine

Available from ARCHWAY Paperbacks

FEAR STREET®
R·L·STINE

College
Weekend

A Parachute Press Book

AN ARCHWAY PAPERBACK
Published by POCKET BOOKS
New York   London   Toronto   Sydney   Tokyo   Singapore

This book is a work of fiction. Names, characters, places and incidents are products of the author's imagination or are used fictitiously. Any resemblance to actual events or locales or persons, living or dead, is entirely coincidental.

AN ARCHWAY PAPERBACK *Original*

An Archway Paperback published by
POCKET BOOKS, a division of Simon & Schuster Inc.
1230 Avenue of the Americas, New York, NY 10020

Copyright © 1995 by Parachute Press, Inc.

ISBN: 0-671-86840-3

First Archway Paperback printing July 1995

10 9 8 7 6 5 4 3 2 1

FEAR STREET is a registered trademark of Parachute Press, Inc.

AN ARCHWAY PAPERBACK and colophon are registered trademarks of Simon & Schuster Inc.

Cover art by Bill Schmidt

Printed in the U.S.A.

IL 7+

College
Weekend

prologue

"**M**iss me?"

"Well, yeah. You know the answer to that."

"But you could say it, couldn't you?" Tina teased, twisting the phone cord between her slender fingers.

"Which train are you coming on?" Josh changed the subject.

Tina sighed. "I told you three times, Josh. The late one. I have to wait for Holly."

Josh grunted. Holly and Josh didn't really get along. Nothing too serious. Josh just thought Holly talked too much, mainly about herself.

How did Holly feel about Josh? Tina wasn't

quite sure. Holly was her cousin. Holly would never say anything bad about a boyfriend of Tina's.

"We'll have a lot of time together, Josh," Tina said. "The whole weekend."

"Great," Josh replied. "I can't wait. I think you'll like my friends, Tina. They're good guys. They know all about you already."

In her dresser mirror Tina caught herself smiling. "You talk about me to your friends?"

"Yeah. Sometimes," Josh confessed. "I have your pictures in my room. People ask me about them."

"I can't wait to be there!" Tina exclaimed. "My first college weekend. Living in a dorm. Hanging out with college kids. And you, of course. You'll meet us at the train station?"

"I'll be there," Josh replied. "No problem."

No problem.

Strange how sometimes simple plans like Tina's go wrong.

No problem.

Those were Josh's words.

But he was wrong.

There were problems.

More problems than either of them could have imagined.

chapter
1

*T*ina Rivers checked her watch for about the millionth time. She wished she could jump out and help pull the train into Patterson Station.

She hadn't seen her boyfriend, Josh Martin, since Christmas. Three long months.

"Wake up, Holly," Tina demanded, nudging her cousin gently on the arm. "We're almost to the station."

Holly Phillips sprawled in the seat next to Tina. Her curly brown hair fell across her face. She snored lightly. "Wake up," Tina coaxed. "Parties are starting, Holly. Parties filled with cute college guys all for you."

Holly groaned as she stretched out her long legs. Finally she opened her eyes and yawned. "College guys?"

"I knew that would get you." Tina turned away from her sleepy cousin and peered anxiously out the window.

Someday I'll be able to travel by myself, Tina thought, remembering the argument with her parents.

Tina begged her mom and dad to let her travel alone to visit Josh. But no. Either her cousin went with her, or Tina stayed home. And no way could Tina miss the Spring Fling Weekend with Josh.

"Do you see him yet?" Holly asked, rubbing her eyes.

"No. It's too dark," Tina answered, reaching into her purse for her makeup bag. "Besides, we're still moving."

She pulled out her lipstick, a mirror, and a brush.

"My stomach is doing flip-flops," Tina said as she brushed out her long blond hair. "Do I look okay?"

Holly sighed. "Five hours on a train, and you look terrific. I feel like a sack of oatmeal next to you."

Tina laughed. "What does a sack of oatmeal feel like?"

"Someday you're going to be a famous model, Tina," Holly told her. "I just know it."

Someday Tina *did* want to be on the cover of fashion magazines. She constantly studied the competition, making plans. But right now she couldn't think about anything except Josh. She missed him so much.

Last year, at Shadyside High, they ate lunch together every day. Now she hardly saw him at all.

Tina took one final glance at her makeup and put the mirror away. Then she sprayed her favorite perfume on her wrists and behind her earlobes. She smiled as she imagined her first kiss from Josh.

"I think we're stopping," Holly said. A screeching sound filled the train car.

The loudspeaker crackled. "We are now arriving at Patterson Station. All passengers please remain seated until the train comes to a complete stop."

Tina jumped up. She couldn't sit still a minute longer.

The train jerked under her feet as she started to pull her luggage down from the overhead rack. She fell forward and grabbed Holly's shoulder to keep from landing on the floor.

"Hurry up," Tina urged. "Do you need help?"

"No. I can get everything," Holly answered,

still sitting. "I'm just stiff. I must have slept funny."

Tina rolled her eyes. Obviously, Holly planned to take her time getting off the train. But then, Holly wasn't in love. She had no clue how eager Tina was to see Josh.

At the door a gray-uniformed conductor nodded at them. "You girls are the only ones getting off here. So be careful," he warned. "The station is pretty deserted. Don't hang around too long."

"We'll be okay," Tina assured him as she hurried down the steps. "My boyfriend is meeting us."

But the platform stood empty. Tina searched anxiously up and down the long walkway. Where was Josh?

She dropped her suitcase. The train had been delayed. They were an hour late. Maybe Josh got tired of waiting and went someplace to get a cup of coffee. That made sense, but still Tina couldn't help feeling disappointed.

If I was meeting Josh, she thought, I'd stand on the platform no matter how late he arrived. I wouldn't want to miss one minute of our time together.

"So where is he?" Holly asked.

Tina shrugged. "You know Josh. He can never stand still. I'm sure he'll be right back."

"Are you sure we're at the right station?" Holly asked.

"Of course," Tina snapped.

The platform started to tremble as the train pulled out. The train left with a roar and the smell of diesel. The girls huddled together on the dark platform.

Holly shook her head. "I hope this isn't a sign of how the whole weekend's going to be."

"Please," Tina pleaded, twisting a strand of hair. "You and your signs. I'm buying you a turban and a crystal ball for your birthday. Then you can have a fortune-telling booth at the Shadyside fair next month."

Holly forced a smile. "You can make fun if you want to, but sometimes I just get these feelings . . . Hey, do you think there are any good dance clubs here?" Holly asked, changing the subject. "It's going to be so cool. No parents. No curfew. I can stay out as late as I want to."

"I can't believe my parents insisted you come with me. If they only knew how evil you really are. You're a very bad influence on me!" Tina joked.

"You love it!" Holly replied.

Tina raised her eyes to the night sky. A single star shone down, pale yellow against the gray.

The first star of evening, Tina thought. The Wishing Star.

She shut her eyes and made a silent wish.

"I wish this will be the best weekend of my life."

A cool wind blew across the platform. Tina opened her eyes and pulled her blue jacket tight across her chest. Josh liked the jacket. But now she wished she'd picked something warmer.

"Let's go inside," she suggested.

Tina grabbed her suitcase and pushed open the big double doors to the tiny station. Tina's suitcase felt as if it weighed a ton. I shouldn't have brought so many different outfits, she thought, dragging it inside. But Josh told her they were going to a picnic, a carnival, and the dance. She needed to be prepared.

But she wasn't prepared for spending time in this empty, grimy train station, in the middle of nowhere. How could Josh do this to me? Tina wondered.

The room smelled musty and sour. Rows of high-backed, gray leather chairs filled the room. Scraps of paper fluttered across the floor, as if pushed by ghosts.

Holly dropped her suitcase and sighed. "Josh knows we're coming, right?"

"Of course," Tina shot back tensely.

"Maybe he forgot or something," Holly said, glancing around the dimly lit room. "Now that he's in college, he might be different. I know I'm going to be different when I'm in college. I'm getting my nose pierced, definitely. And maybe a tattoo."

"I don't think Josh is off getting his nose pierced. I'm going to call him. You wait with our stuff." Tina dug through her purse for a quarter and hurried over to the two pay phones.

She picked up the receiver on the first phone, then slammed it down. "No dial tone!" she yelled to Holly.

The other phone didn't even have a receiver. Tina strode back to her cousin.

"Let's go to the ticket counter," Tina suggested, trying to sound cheerful. "Maybe there's a message for us."

Their footsteps echoed on the tile floor.

A handwritten sign on the counter read BE RIGHT BACK. Next to the sign sat a cup of old coffee.

"Yuck," Holly groaned. "Looks like no one has been here for days."

Tina heard a sound behind the counter. "What's that?" she asked, grabbing Holly's arm. "Listen."

The soft scraping sound grew louder. Tina held her breath.

"An animal," Holly guessed, inching her way around the counter.

9

"Get back," Tina ordered. "It might be a rat."

This place is dirty enough, Tina thought. I bet dozens of rats live here. She tugged her cousin's arm.

Something hit the counter with a heavy thud. Tina spun around.

A huge black cat stared at her. The fur on its tail stood straight up. Its yellow eyes gleamed.

Tina uttered a shriek as it hissed and then hurled itself off the counter.

The cat landed beside Tina's foot and dashed across the floor.

Tina let out a tense laugh. "I—I thought it was the world's biggest rat!"

"A black cat," Holly murmured. "You know what that means."

"It means Josh better get here soon. And that's all it means," Tina declared. "No more signs, okay? I'm not in the mood."

"Let's sit down," Holly suggested.

"Good idea. My knees feel as if they're made of cottage cheese."

"That's because you eat so much of it," Holly teased.

Tina followed her cousin to the stiff-backed chairs. "What time is it now?" she asked.

"Nine," Holly told her. "Josh knows it's tonight he's supposed to pick us up, right?"

"Yes, Holly. Yes, he knows it's tonight. Yes, he knows it's this station. Okay?"

"Okay, okay. Sorry," Holly apologized.

Moonlight streamed through the windows, casting long shadows on the walls.

Tina kept her eyes on the entrance. Please, Josh. Get here soon.

Her mind rushed over a million possibilities.

Maybe she *did* tell Josh the wrong time.

Maybe she *did* get the date wrong.

Maybe . . .

Stop, she ordered herself.

Tina couldn't sit still. She stood up and started to pace around the room. After making a complete circle, she noticed a shadow move outside the window at one end of the station.

"There he is!" Tina cried.

She picked up her bag and hurried to the door. "Josh!" Tina shouted, waving her arm. "Here we are."

"Where'd he go?" Holly asked. "I don't see anyone."

The long platform stood empty.

"Josh!" Tina cried out again.

No one there.

A knot formed in the pit of Tina's stomach. Something wasn't right. "Let's go back inside," she whispered to Holly.

Too late.

A man jumped out from the shadows beside the station.

"Hey—what's up?" he rasped.

"W-we're leaving," Tina stammered.

The man moved in on her. "No, you're not," he said in a low, cold voice. "You're not going anywhere."

chapter

2

"*I* need money," he growled at Tina. "Whatever you got."

Okay, she thought. Okay. He wants money. He can have everything. The whole fifty dollars Dad gave me. Tina fumbled for her purse.

The man jerked his face closer. His hair fell in dirty clumps onto his forehead. His breath smelled of alcohol. His eyes were glassy.

Tina backed against the wall. Her whole body shook.

"My . . . my money's in my . . ." Tina stammered.

But she never finished her sentence.

"Hey—leave her alone!" a deep voice ordered. "Get out of here!"

Josh! Tina thought. Finally!

The man let out a startled cry and lurched away.

Tina covered her face with her hands, ordering her body to stop trembling.

"Are you okay?" her rescuer asked.

That's not Josh's voice, Tina realized.

She raised her eyes to see a stranger with piercing green eyes and dark hair tied in a short ponytail.

"I'm okay—now," Tina told him. "Holly? Holly?"

Holly stood huddled against the station wall, her arms wrapped around herself. Tina rushed to her side. "You okay?"

Holly nodded. "How about you? Did he hurt you?"

"No. He just scared me to death," Tina replied. "I'm going to kill Josh for being late."

Holly turned to the stranger. "Thanks for chasing that guy away."

Tina felt the boy staring at her. His gaze traveled from her face to her legs and then back to her face.

"You must be Tina," he said. "I'm Chris Roberts. Josh's roommate."

"Oh, yeah," Tina replied. "Josh told me about you."

Josh had told her that Chris had tons of money. But Josh had never told her how handsome Chris was.

"Where *is* Josh?" she asked, forcing her eyes away from Chris and around the station. "How come he's not here?"

"He went upstate yesterday on a geology camping trip with our friend Steve," Chris answered.

"Huh? He went camping?" Tina cried. "But he knew I was coming!"

"They were supposed to be back today," Chris explained. "But they called this afternoon from a garage. They had car trouble. They have to wait to get the transmission fixed."

"When will they be back?" Holly asked.

"Later tonight."

"Oh," Tina murmured, disappointed. One whole night knocked off her perfect weekend. But at least now she knew why Josh wasn't here.

"Josh asked me to come get you. Sorry I'm so late," Chris apologized.

"Don't be sorry," Holly said. "If you ask me, you got here just in time." She pushed her curly brown hair away from her face and smiled.

"How did you know it was me?" Tina asked.

"Josh has pictures of you all over our room," Chris explained, staring at her. "All the guys notice them." He grinned playfully.

Tina felt him checking her out again.

"I thought you were coming by yourself," he said, his smile fading.

"I planned to," Tina lied. She didn't want a cool guy like Chris to know her parents didn't let her travel alone. "But Holly wanted to check out the drama department at Patterson. So she came, too."

"Ahem." Holly coughed theatrically.

"Oh, I'm sorry," Tina said. "I didn't introduce you. This is Holly Phillips, my cousin."

"Hi," Chris said without really looking at Holly. "Let's get going." Chris picked up Tina's suitcase. "My Jeep is out front."

Tina followed Chris around the station and over to his car. In a few more hours she'd be with Josh.

Chris shoved the bags in the back of his Jeep Cherokee. Then Holly and Tina climbed in.

As they pulled out of the parking lot, Tina studied the interior of the Jeep. She noted an expensive CD player and even a car phone. Chris must be really rich, she decided.

She rested her head on the plush leather headrest. This is much better than the stiff train seat, she thought.

"So how far to the campus?" Holly asked, poking her head between them from the backseat. "I can't wait to see it. Anything fun going on tonight? Last week I visited Blaine College. They have some great music clubs. But I didn't really like their drama department. Too serious."

Tina shared an amused glance with Chris.

"And last month I went to Munroe College," Holly rambled on. "Can you believe they only put on two plays a year? Plus, the nightlife there was dead."

"Look to your left, Holly," Chris said. "There's the Little Town Playhouse." He pointed to a small brick building set back from the street. "The college drama department performs there sometimes."

"Cute building," Holly said.

Chris leaned over and slid in a CD. A second later a familiar song began playing. "I love this CD," he said, smiling at Tina.

Bizarre! She loved this CD, too. No one she knew, including Josh, had ever heard of the Psycho Surfers, and Chris had their CD.

"You know this group?" Tina asked.

"Sure," Chris answered. "I've played this song so much Josh will only let me listen to it in the car."

"Does this town ever get any concerts?" Holly asked. "Anybody good ever play here?"

"Not too often," Chris replied, turning the Jeep onto a narrow cobblestone street.

"Too bad," Holly answered, slumping back in the seat.

"Holly, check that out," Tina said, pointing to a line of kids outside a club. "There's a place for you."

"That's Club Cobalt. I don't go there much anymore," Chris said. "But it's pretty popular."

Tina noticed a catch in his voice. Why didn't he go there anymore? she wondered.

Holly sighed. "We need more clubs back home, don't we, Tina?"

Tina shrugged. She didn't go out to clubs very often. Without Josh, why bother?

"Tina," Chris said, "Josh told me you want to be a model."

"I do. Ever since I won a modeling contest in the fifth grade," Tina replied.

"Then I'm sure you've heard of my uncle— Rob Roberts, the photographer?" Chris asked.

Rob Roberts! Everyone knew him. Fashion magazines used his model photos on their covers all the time.

"He's your uncle? Wow!" Tina exclaimed, surprised that Josh had never mentioned it to her.

Chris nodded. "I want to work with him after

graduation. He promised he'd help me get started in the business."

"That's great," Tina said.

"If you have time while you're here, I'll do some fashion shots of you," Chris offered. "I need some more stuff for my portfolio."

"That would be a lot of fun, but I don't know if there will be enough time." Actually, Tina hoped there wouldn't be *any* time. She really wanted to spend every minute with Josh.

"I'd love to try some head shots at least," Chris said. And then added: "If there's time."

They rode through the small town. Tina thought about Josh. Holly commented on the stores and restaurants.

"Are you two hungry?" Chris asked, turning onto a one-way street.

"No," Holly replied. "We ate sandwiches on the train."

"Too bad," Chris replied. "There's an awesome Mexican restaurant over there."

Tina smiled. "I love Mexican food."

"Have you ever had a crab enchilada?" he asked.

"Crab?" She raised her eyebrows. "No. Are they good?"

"Great," he answered. "You should go there this weekend."

Tina stared out the window at the starry night. "Josh hates Mexican food," she murmured.

"He doesn't know what he's missing," Chris said.

I know, Tina thought. Me. Josh should be here with me right now.

"This is the dorm," Chris said, pulling the Jeep into a parking space.

Finally, Tina thought, opening the door. Be there, Josh. Be there. The words repeated in her mind as she followed Chris into the tall redbrick dorm.

But when Chris unlocked the room, it stood dark and empty.

"The plan is for you to stay here in our room," Chris told them. "Josh and I got permission from the RA. We'll sleep at my studio."

"Do you think Josh is there now?" Tina asked.

"I doubt it," Chris answered, checking his watch. "It's only ten."

"Why don't we call—just to make sure," Tina suggested. She knew he wouldn't be there. If he'd made it back to town, he would be here waiting for her.

While Chris dialed the number, Tina chewed nervously on the inside of her cheek.

As she expected, no one answered at the studio. Tina flopped down on one of the beds.

She knew she'd see Josh soon. But she couldn't help but feel disappointed.

"See you guys later," Chris said, hanging up the phone. "If you need anything, call me." He wrote the number of the studio on a piece of paper.

"These dorm rooms are bigger than the ones at Blaine College," Holly said, after Chris had left. "And look, they even have a stereo and a TV." She picked up the remote and flipped through the channels until she found MTV.

"I'm sure that stuff belongs to Chris," Tina said. Josh could barely afford to live away from home.

Tina glanced around the room. Two beds, two dressers, and two desks filled most of the space. Josh's old computer sat on his desk. Chris's desk had a color Mac with CD-ROM and a laser printer.

Tina wondered whether Josh ever felt jealous of Chris. If he did, he never mentioned it to her.

Geology maps covered the wall near Josh's bed. A photo of the ocean and an announcement for a photography contest hung on the opposite wall.

And of course, rocks and fossils were perched everywhere. On Josh's desk. On his dresser. On the window ledge. Even on the floor. In every shape and size.

Just like his room at home, she thought. He probably even dreams about rocks.

She picked up a triangular black stone and rubbed it between her fingers. Its rough edge scraped her skin.

Holding the rock, she stood up and paced around the room. Although everything appeared normal, something wasn't right. Something was missing.

"What's wrong?" Holly asked.

"I don't know," Tina answered, tossing the rock onto Josh's bed.

Then it hit her. Where were all the photos of her that Chris had mentioned?

Their prom picture sat on Josh's dresser. But that was it. She picked up the photo and gazed at Josh's handsome face.

Tina knew she would never forget that night. In place of a regular corsage Josh had given her one made out of layers of green mica crystals. It made her feel really special. All night long her friends commented on it.

She turned the photo over to read the inscription on the back.

The writing was gone! How weird, she thought.

She had written a message to him on the back of this photo. Did Josh erase it?

Someone pounded on the door.

Tina hurried to open it. Please be Josh, she thought.

Instead a dark-haired girl stood in the hallway.

"No!" the girl shrieked. "I don't believe it!"

chapter

3

*T*ina stared at the girl. "Excuse me?"

She wore tight blue jeans over a beige bodysuit. Her short dark hair framed her round, serious face.

"I'm so sorry," the girl apologized. "I thought you were someone else. But your hair is much lighter." She blinked rapidly.

"Are you okay?" Tina asked.

"I don't know what's wrong with me," the girl replied. "Too much coffee, I guess. I've really been cramming for exams. And I—I didn't expect you to look like her."

"Like who?" Tina demanded.

"Uh . . . no one," she stammered, waving her

hands in front of her. "Sorry. I'm not making any sense—am I?"

She's lying, Tina thought. What's her problem?

"Who are you?" she asked.

"I'm Carla Ryan," the girl explained. "I've been going out with Steve. You're Tina, right? Chris said he planned to pick you up at the station."

"Right," Tina answered. "And this is my cousin Holly."

Tina relaxed a little. Josh had told her about Steve and Carla. Steve studied geology, too. Carla majored in journalism, and always exaggerated and made an issue out of everything.

"Who do you think I look like?" Tina repeated.

Carla ignored her. She flopped down on Josh's bed. Tina sat next to her.

"I went to high school with Steve and Chris," Carla explained, running her fingers through her short, silky hair. "They're great guys."

"So do you have your own apartment?" Holly asked eagerly as she unpacked her clothes.

"No, not yet," Carla replied. "I live in the dorm. On the tenth floor. But I work at a boutique, and next year I'm getting my own place. I'm sick of the dorm."

I wish I could go away to school next year, Tina

thought. Maybe if I get some modeling jobs, I can afford to go somewhere besides Waynesbridge Junior College.

She didn't care if she lived in a dorm for four years. It *had* to be better than staying at home.

Music blared out from the next room, drowning out the TV.

"You can always tell when it's Friday night." Carla banged on the wall.

The music grew louder. Carla rolled her eyes, and they all laughed.

"If you want to be a model like Josh says, you should get Chris to take some photos of you," Carla suggested. "He's really talented."

"He offered to do it this weekend," Tina said.

"Then you should let him," Carla replied. "Maybe you'll get an agent like my friend in New York. Chris shows his photos to his uncle. He told you about his uncle, right?"

"Uh-huh." Tina checked the clock on the dresser. Five after eleven. Josh should be back soon. "But I want to spend all my time with Josh."

Carla shook her head. "I can't believe Josh went camping. I mean, I see Steve all the time," she said. "But you haven't seen Josh since Christmas break. And with the car trouble, he won't be back till late."

Tina groaned. "Don't remind me."

"Isn't it hard being so far apart?" Carla asked. "I don't know if I could do that with Steve."

"We talk on the phone a lot," Tina explained.

But if he missed her as much as she missed him, why did he go camping this week? His dumb rocks couldn't be that important.

"Did you know they were going?" she asked Carla.

"Of course," Carla replied. "Steve tells me everything."

"Oh," said Tina. Josh used to tell her everything, too. Maybe college did change people.

"Tell us about Chris." Holly finished unpacking and opened a bottle of nail polish. "Does he have a girlfriend?"

"That's a sad story," Carla said softly. She glanced over at the picture of the ocean. "Really sad."

"Don't keep us in suspense," Holly urged as she painted her thumbnail a bright red.

Carla took a deep breath and began. "Back in high school Chris had a girlfriend. Judy. They were totally nuts about each other. I mean, they went everywhere together. They loved to go sailing all the time on Chris's boat. And then last summer . . ."

Carla hesitated. "Last summer they had an accident. They were out really far when a storm suddenly came up. Judy fell overboard and . . ."

"Don't tell me she drowned!" Holly cried.

Carla nodded.

How awful, Tina thought. She couldn't even imagine how she'd feel if something like that happened to Josh.

"Chris tried to save her," Carla continued. "But he couldn't find her anywhere. They had to search for her body for two days."

A heavy silence filled the room. Tina pictured Chris on the boat, the wind whipping the sails, searching, searching for his girlfriend. Horrible.

"Poor guy," Holly muttered, breaking the silence.

"Steve tried to fix him up a couple of times," Carla told them. "But Chris isn't interested."

"Why don't you go out with him, Holly?" Tina asked. She glanced at her cousin.

Holly shook her head. "Not my type," she muttered.

"Too normal?" Tina teased.

"Exactly," Holly replied.

Carla glanced at her watch. She pressed her lips together and shook her head. "I'm going to have a talk with Josh when they get back." She picked up one of Josh's rocks. "I don't think he appreciates you."

Tina watched Carla as she tossed the rock into the air and then caught it. Carla talked as if she knew something about Josh. Something that

Tina didn't know. And it made Tina feel uncomfortable.

Someone knocked on the door.

Holly opened it and Chris walked in. "I forgot I wanted to take my chemistry notes to the studio. What's up, Carla?" he asked.

"Nothing," she answered. "We're just waiting for the guys."

"Any word?" Chris sat down in Josh's desk chair.

Tina shook her head. "I'm getting worried."

"Don't," Carla insisted. "It's pretty foggy out tonight. They'll have to take it really slow. I don't think they'll get back until after midnight."

"Carla's right," Chris added. "Listen, how about going to a party, instead of hanging around here waiting?"

"Good idea," Holly called out.

"I don't know," Tina murmured.

"Come on," Chris urged. "Josh wouldn't want you to get bored."

Tina thought for a moment. Time would go by faster at a party. And when it ended, Josh would be back.

"Okay. Let's go," she told Chris.

"Great," Chris replied. "How about you, Carla?"

Carla shrugged. "Why not?"

"Let me just get changed." Holly picked up a

pair of jeans and a bright red sweater from the bed. "Where's the bathroom?"

"Down the hall," Carla instructed. "Out the door and to your left."

Tina opened up her suitcase. "I need to hang up a few things first."

She pulled out the two outfits she had brought for the dance. A sexy black dress and a miniskirt with a white blouse. She planned to wear the one Josh liked best.

As she shook out the wrinkles, she could feel Chris watching her. Her skin prickled.

With the outfits draped over her arm, Tina opened up the closet door.

She reached for an empty hanger. Her foot bumped into something heavy.

She stared down. That's weird, she thought.

Josh's hiking boots?

If he's on a hike looking for rocks, she wondered, why did he leave them behind?

chapter

4

"Aren't you ready yet?" Holly asked, entering the room. She wore jeans with holes in the knees and a tight red sweater. Beaded earrings dangled almost to her shoulders. "Why are you just standing there?"

"I'm ready," Tina answered, shutting the closet. But she couldn't shut Josh's boots out of her mind. Why did he leave them in his closet?

"Well, are we going or what?" Holly asked impatiently.

"I have to write Josh a note first," Tina replied. "Chris, where are we going? I'll tell him to meet us." She found a pen and a piece of scratch paper on Josh's dresser.

"To a party over in Old Town," Chris responded, staring at her intently as she wrote. "I don't know the address. Tell him to wait here for us."

Carla shook her head and tsk-tsked. "He doesn't deserve you," she said. "If I hadn't seen my girlfriend in three months, I would be right here waiting for her."

Tina sighed and tried to ignore Carla. But she couldn't help agreeing. A lump formed in the back of her throat as she put the note on Josh's pillow.

"Don't listen to Carla," Chris said. "Josh will be back soon."

"Well, let's not stand here and discuss it," Holly demanded. "Let's go to the party."

When they reached the Jeep, Tina decided to sit in the back with Carla. That way Holly and Chris could talk—and maybe Holly would find out that he *was* her type.

She started to climb in.

"Tina," Chris called. "Sit up front with me, okay? And stop worrying."

So much for that plan, Tina thought, settling into the front seat. She rolled down the window and let the cool air blow back her blond hair. She stared at the clear sky. The stars shone brighter here than they ever did in Shadyside.

Tina pictured Josh cruising through the mountains. But still, she couldn't shake her uneasy feeling.

"Chris," Tina began. Her heart started to beat quicker. "Something seems weird to me. I saw Josh's hiking boots in his closet. Why would he leave them if he went camping?"

Chris's eyes widened. "He bought new ones. Really cool with double-padded ankle supports and soft leather."

"Really?" Tina answered, very relieved. "But Josh is on a tight budget. How could he afford new boots?"

Chris downshifted and turned the corner. "He must not have told you about his job. He's been doing some computer work for the geology lab. The pay is pretty decent."

"I think he did mention it," Tina lied, embarrassed to admit that her boyfriend hadn't told her about the job.

Tina stared out the window.

"I've been lost and alone . . . for so long . . . it's so wrong." The words drifted into the air. That's the Spoiled Rotten CD, she thought. I can't believe Chris has this CD, too.

Tina stared at Chris. He hummed along. I bet he's missing his old girlfriend, she thought.

"Do you have this CD?" he asked. "It took me a while to find it."

"Me, too," Tina replied. "I searched everywhere, and then I finally found a store that carries all sorts of weird stuff."

"What else do you like?" Chris asked.

Before Tina could answer, Holly shouted from the backseat, "This music is so gross! Turn it down."

Chris smiled at Tina. He's one of the coolest guys I've met in a long time, she thought.

They turned down a narrow, tree-lined street and found a parking spot along the curb.

"We're here," Chris announced. He shut off the engine.

As they hurried up the long driveway, Tina heard the thump of a bass guitar.

College kids spilled onto the porch and front lawn.

"Hey, Carla!" a tall boy yelled. "Bill's looking all over for you."

"Well, he's going to have to keep looking!" Carla shouted back, brushing her hair away from her face.

Holly giggled.

This is just what Holly loves, Tina thought. A party and guys to flirt with.

The minute she stepped inside, Tina felt uncomfortable. I bet everyone can tell I'm still in high school, she thought.

Tina noticed a girl in jeans and a vest. She had a silver ring in her nose. Another girl wore a minidress with thigh-high socks that stopped a few inches below the hem.

I wish I had changed my clothes, Tina thought. Everyone is going to think I'm so boring. Preppy Little Miss High School.

Tina followed Chris across the living room. Several guys said hi to him and smiled at Tina. College guys actually noticed her! Maybe she didn't appear as boring as she thought.

Finally they found an empty spot along a far wall near an open window. The cool breeze felt good.

"Excellent party!" Holly exclaimed. She swayed to the music.

"Why don't you and Holly dance," Tina suggested to Chris. She had to shout to be heard. "This is one of her favorite songs."

Chris shrugged. "Well, I don't really—"

"Oh, look!" Carla interrupted. "There's the girl playing the lead in *Our Town*. Come on, Holly, I'll introduce you."

Carla grabbed Holly and dragged her away, leaving Tina alone with Chris.

Tina took a step back. It didn't feel right standing so close to him, even though they were surrounded by people. Her first college party, and instead of being with her boyfriend, she ended up with his roommate.

But that wasn't the worst part. The worst part was that she felt attracted to him.

Tina shifted her weight from foot to foot.

"Want something to drink?" Chris asked. "There's some soda in that cooler over there." He pointed across the room.

"Thanks," Tina answered.

"You stay here," Chris told her. "This place is packed."

Chris forced his way through the crowd. Tina lost sight of him almost immediately. She felt sort of awkward standing all by herself. She was relieved when she finally spotted Chris coming back toward her.

Chris handed Tina a soda, and opened one for himself. He took a long swallow, staring around the room. "I don't go to these parties too often. I used to, but . . ." He shifted his eyes away from her.

Tina reached out and touched Chris's arm, trying to think of something to say. "So you like spicy food?" she blurted out.

"Love it," he answered, smiling.

"You should come to Shadyside with Josh. There's a Mexican restaurant not too far away, in Waynesbridge. I'll bet you can't eat more than one of their jalapeños."

"Oh, I don't know about that. We had a

contest last spring at Old Town Festival. And guess who won?"

"Now, let me see," she teased. "How many did you eat?"

"A dozen," he bragged. "My head nearly exploded."

Tina laughed. It would be fun to show Chris around Shadyside. He was so easy to talk to, and they had a lot in common.

"So are you going to start here in the fall?" Chris asked.

"No. I can't afford to go away to school," Tina replied. "I'll probably go to Waynesbridge Junior College, so I can live at home."

"Too bad," Chris said. "There are some great places around here I could show . . . I mean *Josh* could show you, if you had more time."

A slow song started to play.

"Do you want to dance?" he asked.

"Sure," Tina answered.

They found a spot among the other couples. Tina rested her head on Chris's shoulder as they moved back and forth.

"Your hair smells good," he whispered into her ear.

Tina smiled and snuggled in closer. She could feel his muscles under his shirt.

It felt good to be held. Even by the wrong guy.

When the song ended, Chris led her out on the back porch for some fresh air. A million stars dotted the sky. Tina tilted her head back and stared up at the moon. The smell of freshly cut grass drifted up from the lawn below.

Tina inhaled, then let her breath out slowly.

"It's beautiful here," she observed. "I see why you like this place."

Chris put his arm around her. "Make a wish."

Tina gazed up at the brightest star in the sky. "I wish I'll become a famous model some day," she whispered, imagining herself on the cover of *Glamour* or *Vogue.* Flying around the world on a private jet. Visiting exotic places. With enough money to have everything she ever wanted.

"Maybe I can make that come true," Chris said softly, lifting her chin toward his face. "Let me take some shots for your portfolio."

Tina felt her heartbeat quicken. For a few seconds they stared at each other. Then Chris bent down and kissed her lightly on the lips.

Tina felt her body tingle. She wanted him to kiss her again.

He did.

Tina didn't hear the footsteps behind her until it was too late.

Until a voice cried out, "What's going on here?"

chapter

5

Tina jerked away from Chris. She whirled around to find Carla standing there, her arms crossed in front of her.

"I, uh . . . we . . . were . . ." Tina stammered, shoving her hands in her pockets. Her face felt burning hot.

"Hey—no problem." Carla shrugged.

"We were just talking about leaving," Chris said.

How could I kiss Chris like that? Tina asked herself. In the two years she'd been dating Josh, she'd never cheated on him. She'd never even *thought* about it.

I have to make Carla swear she won't tell, Tina

thought. This is something Josh can never find out about. Even if nothing really happened.

"Yeah. Let's go," Tina said. Now more than ever she wanted to find Josh. "Where's Holly?"

"I don't know." Carla tossed her silky hair out of her eyes.

"Where'd she go?" Tina asked. "Haven't you been with her?"

"For a while. But then a bunch of townies came in and we got separated. She danced with some guy, and that's the last time I saw her," Carla said.

"Townies?" Tina asked.

"You know." Carla waved her hand through the air. "The local kids who don't go to school here. They're pretty geeky."

Tina turned to Chris. "I'm going to look for Holly."

"I'm sure she's fine," Chris reassured her.

"You don't know Holly," Tina answered, imagining the worst.

She hurried back inside. The party had definitely changed. Some older guys had arrived. They passed a paper bag back and forth, taking long slugs from the bottle inside it.

Tina felt someone staring at her. She turned her head. A guy with skeleton tattoos covering his upper arms winked at her. She quickly twisted in the other direction.

The floor vibrated from the loud heavy-metal music. The stuffy air made Tina's head ache. She pushed her way through the dance floor, searching desperately for her cousin.

"Hey," a low voice called. "What's your hurry?"

Tina gazed into the bloodshot eyes of a guy wearing his T-shirt around his head.

"I'm looking for someone," she answered curtly.

"Well, here I am." He laughed, grabbing her around the waist. "Dance?"

"No, thanks." Tina wriggled out of his grasp.

"How about a drink?" he asked, forcing a large mug against her lips.

It tasted bitter. "No, really, that's okay," Tina answered, pushing the mug away.

He grabbed her arm. "Hey, you look pretty good. Come on, just dance with me. One dance. I'm not going to hurt you."

Tina smelled his sour breath. She pulled her arm away and hurried across the room.

There she is, Tina thought, relieved. She spotted the top of Holly's curly hair. "Holly!" she called out. She fought her way across the room. A stranger turned around. Not Holly.

"Did you find her?" Chris asked, stepping up beside Tina. His warm smile made her feel a little better. But only a little.

Tina shook her head. "No, not yet."

"I'll go check in the kitchen," Chris offered. "You go down the hall."

Tina made her way down the narrow hallway. She opened the door to a bedroom. Then slammed it shut after getting angry looks from the couple having an argument inside.

"Sorry," Tina mumbled. But she was only sorry she'd come to the party.

On her way back to the living room Tina heard a girl scream. A loud, piercing shriek.

That's Holly! she thought. I know it is!

She pushed her way to the front door.

She reached the porch as several motorcycles zoomed away. One of the riders was holding a girl with curly brown hair.

"Holly!" Tina screamed. "Come back!" she began, running down the sidewalk. She didn't stop until she reached the corner.

A cold wind picked up, howling through the trees. An empty can rattled down the sidewalk.

Where are they taking Holly?

Stay calm, Tina told herself. Stay calm. Maybe Holly *wanted* to go with them.

But then, why did she scream?

Maybe it wasn't Holly.

There are lots of girls with curly brown hair.

I have to find Chris, she thought. He'll know what to do.

As she started back to the party, Tina spotted something shiny on the sidewalk. It glinted in the moonlight.

What's that? she thought, reaching down.

She picked it up and examined it.

And gasped.

No.

Holly's beaded earring.

chapter

6

*T*ina clutched Holly's earring in her hand. They took her, she realized. They took her away.

Her entire body trembling, she ran up the porch steps and bumped into Carla.

"There you are!" Carla exclaimed. "I've been searching all over for you."

"They took her!" Tina shrieked. "Some guys on motorcycles—they dragged Holly away!"

"Huh?" Carla cried. "What are you talking about?"

"Holly's in trouble!" Tina screamed. "We have to find Chris and go after them."

"Whoa," Carla said, putting a hand on Tina's shoulder. "Calm down. Holly is with a girl named Alyssa Pryor. That's why I was looking for you. To tell you. She's fine."

"Alyssa Pryor?" Tina repeated. "From Shadyside?"

Carla nodded. "Yeah. She said she knew Alyssa from home. And Alyssa's in the drama department, so she took Holly to see the drama building."

"That makes sense," Tina told her. "Holly and Alyssa were in some plays together back home. I forgot Alyssa decided to go to school here."

Tina felt relieved. She could imagine how horrified her parents would be—and Holly's—if they found out she'd lost her cousin.

"But it's after midnight. Why would they go to the drama building now?" Tina asked.

"The drama kids at this school are so weird," Carla replied, rolling her eyes. "I mean they are way strange. Sometimes they hang out at the stage all night."

Tina yawned and sat down next to Carla on the steps. "Are we supposed to wait here for her?"

"No way," Carla answered. "I'm tired. Let's get Chris to take us home."

"But what about Holly?" Tina insisted.

"She'll be with a whole bunch of kids. Don't

45

worry. Someone will give her a ride," Carla reassured her.

Tina sighed. She gazed up at the sky. Clouds had moved in, but Tina spotted a few stars. She picked out the brightest one. This time she wished that Josh was waiting for her back in the dorm. And that she had never, never kissed Chris.

"Listen," she said to Carla. "About what you saw before."

Carla's eyes grew wide. "You're the first girl Chris has been with since the . . . you know . . . the accident."

"It wasn't like that," Tina insisted. "We weren't together."

"You could have fooled me," Carla declared, laughing.

"I have a boyfriend," Tina answered.

"Well, I always say," Carla continued with a grin, "if you can't be with the one you love, love the one you're with."

"Really, Carla," Tina insisted. "Please don't say anything to Josh. Promise?"

"No big deal," Carla murmured. "You know, college isn't like high school. Steve and I see other people. Almost everyone does."

"You do?" Tina asked. "Don't you get jealous?"

"Not really. You'll see."

But Tina didn't see. When she pictured Josh with another girl, her insides turned all funny.

"Please don't say anything," Tina repeated.

"Don't worry about it," Carla said, getting up. "Have fun, Tina. This is your big college weekend!"

Tina didn't feel like talking on the way back to the dorm.

Chris turned on the radio, but Tina couldn't focus on the music. How could Holly go off like that without telling her? And why wasn't Josh here? Why was Carla so anxious for her to be with Chris? And why had she let herself kiss him?

The more she tried to figure it all out, the angrier she became. With Holly. With Carla. With Josh. With herself.

Chris pulled the Jeep up to the curb. Carla climbed out of the backseat before Tina even opened her door.

"See you tomorrow," Carla called and ran into the dorm.

Why is she in such a hurry? Tina wondered. She really is trying to fix me up with Chris.

Tina turned to face him. "Thanks for the ride," she said. "I better go up. I'm sure Josh is back by now."

"I'll go with you," Chris volunteered.

"I'll be fine," Tina answered. "Really."

"I'll just come up for a second," he insisted. "I need to pick up a few things."

Tina's heart beat faster as they entered the dorm and began climbing up the steps to Josh's room.

She opened the door. "Josh?" she called anxiously. But once again she saw the room dark and empty.

Still not back, she realized, sighing unhappily.

She spotted her note on the bed where she had left it. It had not been moved.

The digital clock read one-fifteen.

"Where is he?" she demanded. "Maybe they had an accident."

Chris shook his head. "I'm sure they're fine. They're probably going real slow. It's a scary road in the dark."

"That's why I'm worried," Tina answered.

She checked the answering machine. No messages.

Tina swallowed. This was not like Josh at all. Something wasn't right.

"Do you want to come with me to the studio?" Chris asked.

"No," Tina answered quickly. "I'll stay here and wait. Please go see if he left a message there."

Chris stared into her eyes. He wants to kiss me again, Tina thought.

But instead he smiled.

"I'll call you if there's a message at the studio. And I'll see you tomorrow," he promised. He gave her a quick wave, turned, and left the room.

Ten minutes later the phone rang. Tina rushed to answer it.

"Josh?" she cried. She couldn't wait to hear his voice.

"No. It's me. Chris."

Tina carried the phone over to the bed and stretched out. "Any word?"

"Josh left a message for you here," Chris said.

"What happened? Why didn't he call the dorm?"

"He tried, but the machine is broken," Chris explained. "The garage couldn't get the car part until tomorrow. So they have to spend the night in a dumpy motel."

"Really?" Tina said shrilly, unable to hide her disappointment. "When will they be back?"

"About noon tomorrow. They're about four hours away," Chris told her.

Four hours. They wouldn't be back until lunch. Tina would hardly have any time with Josh.

"Tina, are you there?" Chris asked.

"Yes. Thanks for calling," she said. "See you tomorrow."

Tina hung up the phone. This has to be the worst weekend of my life! she thought angrily. It will probably be *months* before I get the chance to be with Josh again. She heaved the pillow across the room.

Tina changed into a long T-shirt and climbed into Josh's bed. She smelled his aftershave on the sheets. She had never missed anyone so much in all her life.

If Holly hadn't run off, at least I'd have someone to talk to. Tina decided to wait up for her cousin.

She pulled a geology magazine from Josh's bedside table and flipped through, searching for an interesting article. Rocks and minerals! How boring.

She found something on gold mining and started to read. But after only a few seconds the words started to blur, and she felt herself drifting off to sleep.

Yawning, she padded across the room and turned off the light. Then she crawled back in bed.

Cold silver moonlight washed in through the window. The frightening face of the man at the train station flashed before her eyes. She turned away from the window. Think of something else, she ordered herself. But the unfamiliar shapes in the room made her imagination run wild.

This is silly. I'm in a dorm room, perfectly safe.

I'll think about Josh. And only Josh.

About how it feels when he puts his arms around me. About tomorrow when we'll go to the carnival together and ride the Ferris wheel.

Nice thoughts. Restful thoughts. Thoughts that drift into sleep. . . .

What's that noise?

Tina awoke with a start. What time was it? How long had she been sleeping? She didn't want to move, so she couldn't see the clock.

She lay still, holding her breath.

There it was again.

A strange clicking noise.

Someone's here, she thought. Someone is in the room.

chapter

7

T ina sat up, squinting into the darkness. A chill ran down her back.

"Holly—is that you?"

No reply.

"Josh?"

I have to turn on the light, she decided.

But what if someone is in the room with me? What if they grab me when I stand up?

Tina listened hard. She couldn't hear anything but her beating heart. She slid out of bed and stumbled across the carpet.

She flipped on the switch.

Her eyes darted around the room. Empty.

"Wow," Tina muttered. "I must be completely stressed out. I'm hearing things now."

She froze.

The door stood open.

Someone *had* been in her room.

She stepped out into the hall. She glanced up and down the corridor.

No one.

An eerie silence settled over the dorm.

Shaken, Tina slipped back inside. She shut and locked the door.

She grabbed the blanket off the bed, wrapped it around her shoulders, and paced nervously.

I can't believe I left the door unlocked, Tina thought.

Who was in here?

The digital clock read four. Four! And still no Holly. Where was she?

Tina gazed out the window into the night. Dark clouds rolled across the sky. A storm must be coming, she thought, hugging the blanket around her.

Tina pictured Josh asleep in a dumpy old motel room. With cockroaches crawling up the cracked walls.

Serves you right, Josh, she thought. Why did you have to leave this week?

Tina dragged herself over to Josh's desk. She pulled out the chair and sat down.

She spotted her last letter to Josh on the desktop. Tina smiled. He saved it. I hoped he would.

She picked through some receipts for CDs, a pile of change, and a mineral chart. Off to the side lay a research paper on rock formations.

When she picked up the paper, a familiar stone caught her eye.

Isn't that the key chain I gave him last Christmas? she wondered. What is it doing here?

She picked up the rectangular piece of quartz. His keys dangled from the chain.

How could Josh drive upstate without his keys? He always claimed this quartz brought him good luck. He never went rock collecting without it.

"I'll call Chris," she murmured. "He'll have the answer. No, I can't call him now," she argued. "It's the middle of the night."

Oh, great. Now I'm talking to myself, she thought.

Get a grip. Stop being so suspicious. Besides, Josh called earlier.

I'll go back to sleep. That's it. And when I wake up it'll be morning. Everything always looks better in the morning. At least, that's what my mother's told me four thousand times.

She crawled back into bed.

"What's that?" she said out loud.

Something knocked against the window.

Tina gazed into the night. A heavy rain beat against the glass. Lightning flashed across the sky. Thunder crackled through the air.

Tina hugged the blanket closer to her chest.

I bet Holly would say that the storm is a bad sign.

Go to sleep, Tina, she told herself. Don't think. Go to sleep. Don't think. She repeated the words over and over until her eyes fluttered shut.

When she woke up, sunlight streamed into the room. Now, there's a sign. And a good one, she thought. The storm is over.

She glanced at the clock. Ten-fifteen. How could I have slept so late? Josh will be back in two hours!

She turned to the other bed, expecting to find Holly. The bed hadn't been touched.

Holly's clothes remained where she'd left them.

She stayed out all night.

You're not her mother, Tina reminded herself. Holly couldn't wait for this no-curfew weekend.

Well, if Holly isn't going to call me, then I'll have to call her, Tina thought.

She dialed information and asked for Alyssa Pryor's number.

"I'm sorry. There's no listing under that name," a sweet voice replied.

Now what? She decided to call the studio.

"Is Josh back yet?" she blurted into the phone when Chris answered.

"He's not due for a few more hours, Tina," Chris reminded her.

Tina sighed. "I thought maybe he'd call me from the motel this morning."

"He probably thought he'd wake you up. Want me to come by and show you and Holly around the campus?" Chris offered.

"Holly didn't even come home last night."

"She probably crashed with that girl she knows," Chris suggested.

"Maybe," Tina replied, twisting the phone cord.

"Calm down." Chris's soothing voice made her feel better. "Let me just finish developing this one set of proofs and I'll be right over."

"And also, Chris?" Tina started. "I found Josh's keys last night."

"You what?" Chris asked. "I can't hear you. A big truck is passing by. Oh, there's the timer," he said. "I'll be there soon."

Tina stared at the receiver and listened to the dial tone. Chris hadn't even said good-bye.

She pulled on her clothes. Music blared through the wall from the next room.

Tina felt a pang of jealousy. Everyone else is having a good time. Everyone but me. She picked up a piece of green mica.

This is just like my prom corsage, she thought.

She was still gazing at the mica when Chris knocked on the door.

"I thought you might be hungry." He handed her a bag of doughnuts. "I hope you like chocolate."

She did. In fact, they were her favorite.

But she had more important things on her mind than doughnuts.

"Chris, look what I found," she said, picking up Josh's keys. "Didn't you say they took his car?"

"I'm sure he has a spare set," Chris answered quickly.

"But why wouldn't he take the key chain I gave him?" Tina asked. "He said it brought him good luck."

"Maybe he didn't want to lose it," Chris replied. "Or get it scratched. They're camping in a really rough place."

He's right, Tina thought.

She devoured two doughnuts as they walked to the campus.

The sun beat down on Tina's arms. A cool breeze rustled the treetops. Chris took long, slow strides, his arms swinging at his side.

Their fingers touched. Tina stuffed her hands into her pockets. I have to watch myself, she thought. I'm so attracted to him.

"This is fraternity row," Chris explained as they passed several Victorian-style homes.

"Did you try to get into one?" Tina asked. "What do they call it? Did you pledge a fraternity?"

"No," Chris answered sharply. "I'm not into that."

"Neither is Josh," Tina replied.

"Really? Then how come he's pledging next semester?" Chris asked.

"He is?" Tina asked, stunned. She and Josh always agreed that fraternities and sororities were uncool. Has he changed so much? Tina wondered.

"Haven't you guys been talking lately?" Chris asked.

"I think maybe he did mention it," Tina lied.

"Patterson College," Chris announced as they walked up the main steps. "Home of the losing Mavericks. One touchdown a game is their limit."

"Don't they ever win?" she asked.

"Hardly." Chris smiled. "Let's check out the drama department." Chris pointed up a hill. "Sometimes the drama majors sleep in the dressing rooms. Maybe Holly stayed with them."

Chris and Tina hiked up the sloping hill to an impressive brick building.

When they entered, Tina gaped at the high ceiling and long corridors. Posters of famous plays and actors lined the walls.

This is nothing like the tiny drama department back in Shadyside, Tina thought.

They poked their heads into several rooms.

"Anyone here? Holly?" Tina called.

No answer.

"Let's go backstage," Tina suggested.

She dragged Chris through the big auditorium. Their footsteps echoed as they crossed the empty stage.

Someday I'll be modeling on a stage like this, she thought. Strutting down the runway in fancy clothes.

"What are you thinking about?" Chris asked.

"Modeling," she answered.

"You'd be great.", He gazed at her admiringly.

His stare made her nervous and happy at the same time.

"Let's go check the dressing rooms," she urged.

Tina climbed onto the stage and hurried across. She peeked into every dressing room. Wonderful costumes hung on hangers. Long Victorian dresses, capes, torn shirts, ballet outfits.

Then she explored the crowded prop room.

This school definitely has a great drama department, she thought. I bet Holly decides to go here in the fall.

"She's not in a dressing room," Chris called.

"And she's not in here, either." Tina sighed.

They headed for the exit. Tina heard a swishing sound.

She grabbed on to Chris's arm.

A janitor appeared with his broom.

I have to calm down, she thought. I'm so jumpy.

"Now where?" Tina asked.

"Let's try the cafeteria," Chris suggested. "Holly eats—doesn't she?"

Tina laughed. "Sometimes."

They hurried to the other side of the campus. The smell of strong coffee drifted out the cafeteria windows.

Tina ran inside. "Have some drama students been here?" she asked a group of girls at a long table.

They shook their heads. "Not this morning," a girl with long dark hair replied. "But I think there was an all-night party over on Fifth Street."

Tina turned to Chris. "Do you think they went there?"

"Could be," he answered. "But on the weekends there's a party every few feet!"

If only my parents had let me come alone, Tina thought. I'd have been so much better off.

They left the cafeteria. Tina slumped onto the grass. "Now what?" she asked. "We can't drive around the whole town. I know I'm not Holly's baby-sitter. But I'd feel better if I found out where she is."

"Why don't we try calling her friend?" Chris suggested.

"I tried already. It's not listed."

"I can get it," he said. "There's a student directory in the bookstore."

Tina waited while Chris trudged up the hill to the bookstore. She pulled out a blade of grass and twirled it between her fingers. Here she sat on a gorgeous college campus, and she couldn't enjoy herself for a moment.

"Got it," Chris said, interrupting her thoughts. "Here's a quarter."

They found a pay phone. Tina dropped in the quarter and dialed the number. Her spirits lifted. *Alyssa will answer. Holly will have a dumb excuse for not calling.*

But at least I'll know Holly's okay, she thought. *Then I'll go back to the dorm and wait for Josh. He'll be back in an hour.*

After two rings the message machine turned on. "This is Alyssa," a tiny, high-pitched voice began. "I'm onstage right now and can't take your call. Leave your name and I'll—" The machine clicked off in midsentence.

Tina dropped the receiver. It dangled against her leg.

Something was wrong. Tina knew it now for sure.

The voice on the answering machine was not Alyssa Pryor's!

chapter

8

"**S**omething's wrong!" Tina cried. Too many things are wrong, she thought. Too many.

She didn't want to admit it, but Holly's sixth sense could be right this time.

"The machine cut me off. I couldn't even leave a message. And that wasn't Alyssa's voice."

"You know actresses," Chris replied. "They're always goofing around with fake voices and accents. Maybe she's rehearsing for a part."

"Maybe," Tina answered. "But I wanted Holly to know we're looking for her."

"Do you want to call home?" Chris suggested. "You can use my calling card." He pulled out his wallet and began shuffling through his credit cards.

Wow! Tina thought. He has more credit cards than my mom!

"No." Tina wandered back to the grassy area and plopped down. "No, if Holly's off with some guy, I'll just get her in trouble. And then I'll be in trouble, too."

Chris sat beside her, his shoulder almost touching hers. "It's not your fault."

"You don't know our folks," Tina grumbled. "We're supposed to watch out for each other."

A couple strolled by holding hands and laughing. Tina envied them. This is supposed to be the best weekend of my life, she thought. So far it's the worst.

A blue jay chirped in the tree overhead. Tina heard music off in the distance.

"That's the carnival starting up," Chris explained. "It's over in the main quad. You want to check there?"

Tina parted the grass with her finger. "What time is it?" she asked.

Chris checked his watch. "Ten to twelve."

"It's almost twelve?" Tina jumped up. "We should go back to the dorm. Didn't you say Josh would be back around noon?"

Chris didn't answer.

"Chris," Tina prodded. "What's the matter?"

"Is that Carla?" he asked, squinting his eyes.

Carla came rushing up over the grass. Her white T-shirt had PATTERSON MAVERICKS printed across the chest. Sunglasses held her hair back from her face.

"Finally!" she cried. "Where have you two been?"

"Everywhere," Tina answered.

"Josh and Steve called," Carla announced.

"They did!" Tina's heartbeat quickened.

"He tried your room first," Carla explained. "But you were out."

"Well? Where are they?" Tina demanded.

"They're still stuck. The garage fixed the car, but then it broke down again." Carla tucked a stray hair behind her ears. She kept twisting around, staring behind her.

"So anyway, I'm going to drive up there and get them." Carla turned to leave.

"Wait!" Tina grabbed her arm. "I'm going with you."

Carla bit on her lip. Her eyes darted to Chris.

"No," she told Tina. "You can't!"

"**W**hy not?" Tina held on to Carla's arm. She wasn't about to let her leave.

Why is she acting so weird? Tina wondered. She won't even look at me. Josh is my boyfriend. I want to go with her to pick him up.

"You have to take me," Tina insisted.

"There's no room," Carla explained. "I only have a two-seater." She pulled Tina's hand away. "One of the guys is going to have to scrunch down in the window well."

"Oh." Tina sighed. "But Chris has room in his Jeep. How about it?" she asked hopefully.

"Sure," he answered, handing her the keys.

"Carla, you can drive it. I'll hang around in case Holly turns up."

Holly! Tina thought. I shouldn't leave until I know she's okay.

"I'd better stay, too," she told Carla reluctantly. "But get back here quick. And tell Josh I can't wait to see him."

Carla nodded and hurried away. Tina placed her hand on Chris's shoulder. "She sure acted strange, didn't she? I had the feeling she really didn't want me to go with her."

"Maybe she's stopping to visit some guy on the way," Chris said. "With Carla you never know."

Stop and visit another guy? Tina's mouth went dry. Maybe she wants to spend time with Josh. She did say that she and Steve dated other people.

All weekend she's been trying to fix me up with Chris. Suddenly Tina saw things in a whole new light. Maybe Carla was pushing her toward Chris because she's interested in Josh.

"Chris—do you think Carla wants to get together with Josh? Maybe that's why she didn't want me to go?"

"With Steve right there?" he asked.

"No. I guess not. But there's something strange about the way she's been acting to me."

"You worry too much." Chris put his arm

around Tina's shoulders. "Look, you need to have a little fun. I don't want this weekend to be a complete disaster. So here's my idea. A friend of mine owns a motorcycle shop. Let's rent a motorscooter for the day. I'll show you around. And I'll get some outdoor shots for your portfolio."

"What about Holly?" Tina asked.

"We'll keep calling the dorm room while we're out. Maybe we'll even spot her strolling around town."

A half hour later Tina sat on the back of the motorscooter, her arms wrapped around Chris's waist.

As they rode down the old streets, the wind whipped through her hair. Chris stopped the scooter on the top of a hill.

Tina gazed out over the town. The streets wove around in circles. Large maple trees lined the sidewalks. The town ended at the base of a mountain. Snow capped the highest peak.

I wish I could go to school here, she thought. It's so beautiful.

"This is Lookout Point," Chris explained. "I want to get some shots of you here."

He pulled out a pair of wire-rimmed glasses and slipped them on. "I need these to focus," he said shyly.

He looks handsome in glasses, Tina thought.

Chris adjusted his camera settings while Tina stood at the top of the hill.

"Okay," he said finally. "Look out over the town. Let your hair blow free."

He clicked the shutter. "Act natural, Tina."

This is hard, she thought. How can I act natural when Rob Roberts may see these pictures? She didn't know how to position her hands. Or what to do with her feet.

"Relax," Chris coaxed. "Think about tonight. About the dance."

Tina thought about dancing with Josh.

"Great!" Chris exclaimed. "That's exactly what I want." He clicked one shot after another.

He's watching me so carefully, Tina thought. Are all photographers this intense? Or is there something else happening between us?

"Okay," he said, lowering the camera. "That's enough here."

They rode to the library, a large, old stone building with stained-glass windows.

Chris shot several pictures of Tina sitting on the steps. And some of her strolling in front of the entrance columns.

Modeling for someone who knows what he's doing is really fun, she thought.

"These are going to be terrific." Chris took her hand and led her back to the scooter. "You're a natural."

Tina's heart fluttered. "I hope so," she said. "I've wanted to be a model all my life."

For a second he gazed longingly at her. She felt her stomach twist. She was having such a great time, she had completely forgotten about Holly.

"We have to go back to the dorm. What if Holly is there looking for me?"

"No, listen. Let's go to the carnival. It's a natural place for Holly to turn up. She knows that's where you're supposed to be."

"Okay," Tina agreed.

They climbed back on the scooter and started across town.

At a red light Chris jumped off.

Now what's he doing? she thought.

He grabbed his camera and snapped a picture of Tina's startled face.

When the light turned green, he hopped back on. Tina wrapped her arms back around his waist.

I hope these photos come out good, she thought, or I don't want anyone to see them. Especially Rob Roberts.

As they approached the main quad, Tina heard the Spring Fling Carnival in full swing. Excited screams drifted into the air from the tilt-a-whirl and the roller coaster.

The salty-sweet aroma of popcorn and cotton candy greeted her. Chris parked the scooter under a tree. He reached for Tina's hand to help her off.

Boys wearing T-shirts with fraternity names emblazoned on the front called out to them. "Three throws for a dollar! Right here. Win your girlfriend a stuffed bear!"

Tina watched a cute little boy throw a dart into a balloon. He won a huge stuffed bear.

I should be here with Josh, she thought. Chris is being great. Spending all this time with me. But he's not Josh.

"Come on," Chris said, taking her hand. "I want to try the softball toss. I'll win you a prize. How about one of those big purple Barneys?"

"Ugh! No, thanks," Tina protested.

Chris handed his camera to Tina. The attendant gave him three softballs to toss through the rings.

Chris rolled the first ball around in his hands and then aimed for the ring. He made it. Before throwing the second one, he turned and smiled at Tina. The second one also fell through the ring. He winked at her.

Tina held her breath as he tossed the third softball. It hit the side of a ring and fell to the floor.

"Oh, well." He reached in his pocket for more change.

Good, Tina thought. She really didn't want a stuffed Barney.

"Tina?" a deep voice called out.

"Jack!" she exclaimed. "Hi!" Jack Hampton had graduated from Shadyside High a year before Josh.

"What are you doing here?" Jack asked. He stared curiously at Chris. "Aren't you still going with Josh?"

"Of course," Tina answered. "I came here to see him this weekend. But you know Josh. He went off on some geology search and had car trouble."

Jack shook his head. "Sounds like Josh."

"This is Chris." Tina pulled Chris over. "Josh's roommate. He's showing me around."

Jack reached out to shake hands with Chris. Chris clasped Jack's hand briefly.

"We better get going," Chris suggested. "I want to grab some shots at the merry-go-round." He played with the straps of his camera.

He's jealous, Tina thought.

"Just a minute," she said. "I haven't seen Jack in a long time."

"Your folks let you come here alone?" Jack asked. "That's a surprise."

"Hardly," Tina admitted. "I came with my cousin Holly. You haven't seen her around, have you? I think she's hanging out with Alyssa Pryor."

"Alyssa Pryor?" Jack frowned. "From Shadyside?"

Tina nodded. Out of the corner of her eye she saw Chris fidgeting with his camera.

"That's weird," Jack commented. "Alyssa doesn't go here anymore. She transferred to an art school in Seattle."

chapter
_____
10

"That's impossible!" Tina cried. She dug her fingers into Chris's arm. "Are you sure? Alyssa Pryor? With short blond hair? The one whose father owns a clothing store at the mall?"

"I'm positive," Jack replied. "I talked to her on the phone last week. We even talked about you and Josh. About everyone from Shadyside."

Tina's head began to spin.

Someone is lying. And it has to be Carla.

"Then where is Holly?" Tina asked.

She pictured Holly lying in a ditch somewhere. Or tied to a chair, being tortured by drunken bikers.

"Maybe she's with a different Alyssa," Jack suggested.

I don't think so, Tina thought. If only I knew what Carla was up to.

A pretty girl with red hair walked up and looped her arm through Jack's. "Everyone is waiting for you," she cooed.

Jack waved as the girl dragged him away. "Don't worry!" he shouted. "You'll find Holly. Tell her I said hi."

"We have to look for her," Tina urged, turning back to Chris. "Something awful might have happened." She pushed away from the carnival booths and into the crowd.

She bumped into a boy carrying a box of popcorn. She spun around the other way. A clown jogged toward her. His full red lips reminded Tina of blood. Several small children followed the clown. They circled Tina's legs, laughing and shouting.

She felt trapped. Get away from me! she thought. I can't think. I need space.

She cupped her hands over her ears. Holly— where *are* you? "I have to get out of here!" Tina cried.

"Calm down," Chris said. He took her arm and led her to a bench.

"How can I be calm?" she shouted. "My cousin is missing. She could be anywhere. And that strange voice on the phone machine sounded so creepy. Something is totally wrong."

Chris adjusted his ponytail. "You said that Holly wants to be on her own, right?" He stared into her eyes. "And that she's always out for a good time?"

"Yes, but . . ." Tina stopped talking. I know he's trying to be reasonable, she thought. And I promised myself not to get upset again. But this is different. This time I know someone's lying. "We have to call the police."

"You can't file a missing-persons report until someone's gone for twenty-four hours. It's only been . . ." Chris checked his watch. "It's only two. You guys didn't get here until nine last night."

Is that all? Tina thought. I feel as if I've been waiting forever for Josh. "Maybe I should call my aunt and uncle," she mumbled.

"If you want," he answered.

No, I don't really want to, she thought. They would call her parents and everyone would show up in Patterson. And her weekend with Josh would be over before it began.

"No," she said, swinging her foot back and forth on the concrete. "I don't know what to do."

"I know what you need," Chris said. He slapped his hands on his thighs. "How about a frozen banana?"

Of all the food at a carnival, frozen bananas were Tina's favorite. How does he keep doing that? Tina thought. Is he a mind reader or something?

"Okay," she agreed halfheartedly.

They weaved among the booths and rides to the ice-cream stand. Tina's mind drifted away from the carnival. I'm not being fair to Chris, she thought. He certainly hadn't asked to spend all weekend with me. I have to stop thinking and just have a good time.

After frozen bananas, they headed for the Ferris wheel. As they stood in line, Tina tried to keep up her half of the conversation. But her mind kept wandering to Holly and Josh.

"So have you heard of them?" Chris asked.

"Heard of who?"

"Never mind," Chris replied. "We're next."

The attendant led them to a car. Chris lowered the safety bar. A minute later the ride began. The balmy spring air brushed against her face. The sounds faded into the distance.

Tina's stomach fluttered when the car swooped down. She felt a rush as the car lifted back in the air.

Chris fiddled with the settings on his camera. He focused on Tina and took several shots as they rode around.

Tina searched the crowd below, hoping to see

Holly. On the way down next time, she thought, I'll check another section.

But the car didn't go down another time. It jerked and then came to a stop.

Tina glanced up at the open sky. I can almost touch the clouds, she thought.

"We're stuck," Chris said. "Have you ever been stuck at the top before?"

"No," Tina answered.

The children in the car below began crying for their parents.

A bird landed on one of the spokes of the giant wheel, then flew away.

I wish I could fly away, Tina thought, and start this weekend all over again.

Deep in thought, she didn't realize Chris had moved closer—until he draped his arm around her. His eyes locked on hers.

Not now, she thought. I can't kiss him up here. I can't kiss him at all. I have a boyfriend. A boyfriend who will be back any minute.

Tina edged away.

Chris ran his hand along her cheek. "Stop worrying," he said soothingly. "I told you you worry too much." He wrapped his arms around her and leaned forward.

Then he pressed his soft lips on hers. She didn't want to, but she couldn't help herself. She gave in and returned the kiss.

Chris held her tighter. His kisses grew deeper.

I like this, she thought. I know I shouldn't, but I really do.

A gentle breeze rocked the car. The screaming children faded into the distance.

Chris ran his fingers through her hair.

Then he cupped her face in his hands. A faraway look came over his eyes.

"Chris." Tina touched his arm. "Are you all right?"

He didn't answer.

"Chris," she repeated. "Say something."

He narrowed his eyes at her.

What is he seeing? she wondered. His expression is so cold.

Chris removed the rubber band from his ponytail. His hair fell down his neck. He shook it out.

"Sorry," he finally said. "It's just that I haven't been on a Ferris wheel since . . ." His voice drifted off.

"It's okay," Tina replied softly. "Carla told me about her."

"I keep seeing her face," Chris murmured. "I wish I could shut it out."

"It takes time," Tina said. It felt good to comfort Chris. After all, he'd been reassuring her all day.

He turned his piercing green eyes on her. "You know, Josh is a fool for leaving like that," he declared. "What if I hadn't arrived at the train station when I did? Do you know what might have happened to you?"

Tina shuddered. "Don't remind me."

"He should have stayed here," Chris continued. "I told him if I had a girlfriend like you, I wouldn't go anywhere."

He moved closer.

"I hope they get this thing fixed," Tina said, peering down.

"What's the hurry?" Chris slid his arm around her again.

"I'm afraid of heights," Tina lied.

He held her tightly. Her bones pressed into his chest. She could hardly breathe.

Please, start this ride back up. Please. We're too heavy to be on one side of the car.

Tina gazed down to the ground below.

Chris forced his lips on hers. He tasted like chocolate and bananas. *I don't want to kiss him anymore,* she thought.

"Chris!" Tina cried, pushing him away. "Please. We're tilting the car."

Chris pressed his mouth against hers.

She turned her face away. "Stop," she said firmly.

"What's wrong?" Chris snapped. "What kind of game are you playing?"

"I-I'm not playing any game," Tina stammered.

Chris grabbed her and planted a slobbery kiss on her cheek. He ran his tongue inside her ear. Chills shot down her body.

"Stop it!" she shouted. "I mean it." She shoved him to the other side of the car.

Please start this ride. Please!

"I thought you felt something for me," Chris said angrily. "A minute ago you didn't seem to mind kissing me. Admit it, you feel something!"

"I do . . . I mean, I like you, but you know how I feel about Josh."

"What about last night?" Chris protested. "And a few minutes ago? You weren't thinking about Josh then."

I need to find the right words, Tina thought. "You're right," she began. "But Josh and I have been together for two years." She swallowed hard.

Chris's eyes darted around the car. He put his hands on the safety bar and began rocking.

"I'll tip this thing over," he threatened. "You're a tease, aren't you! Admit it, Tina!"

The car tilted forward.

"Chris!" Tina cried. "Stop. We're going to fall out."

"Then kiss me," he insisted, moving closer.

"Kiss me and then tell me how you feel. Go ahead. Kiss me now!"

"No!" Tina shouted.

Chris used his weight to swing the car.

Back and forth. Back and forth.

"Stop!" she demanded.

Tina felt her stomach drop. Her blood rushed to her head. She gripped the safety bar.

Tina stared at the crowd below. She pictured herself falling . . . falling. Splattered on the cement.

"Chris! Are you *crazy?*" she shrieked.

Chris laughed. He gave the car another hard swing.

Tina's pulse raced.

She opened her mouth to scream. Nothing came out.

Her fingers slipped off the safety bar.

Chris swung the car harder.

I'm falling, she thought.

I'm going to die!

She shut her eyes and started to fall.

chapter

11

Down . . . down.

No. Not falling.

The car was moving again. The Ferris wheel had started to turn.

The car swung upright. Tina breathed a long sigh of relief. She turned to Chris.

He toyed with the strap of his camera. He stared silently ahead.

What's he thinking? Does he realize he nearly killed us?

Still shaking, Tina hugged the far corner of the car. Down they swooped. She leaned forward, ready to jump off as soon as their car stopped.

It didn't. Now what's happening? she thought.

"Hey, Chris!" The attendant waved. "I'll give you a couple more spins since you were stuck up there for so long."

No, Tina thought. I have to get away from him.

"How about some more photos?" Chris asked casually. He pulled his camera out of the case.

He's acting as if nothing happened, Tina thought. I can't believe this.

"The lighting up here is terrific," he said. He caught her frightened expression. "I scared you, huh?"

Tina nodded.

"I'm sorry," he mumbled. He fiddled with the settings. "I was only joking. I really am sorry."

His voice sounded sweet again. More like the Chris who had been helping her all weekend.

I feel sorry for him, she thought. His girlfriend's death must have really flipped him out.

Tina remained silent as the car continued to circle. Get me off this thing, she thought. Then I'll deal with Chris.

Finally the car reached the ground and stopped.

Tina stumbled off.

"Hey, wait up!" Chris called, chasing after her. He grabbed her arm. "Tina," he pleaded softly. "Don't be angry. Please."

Tina sighed. He appeared so lost.

If I hadn't kissed him in the first place, none of this would have happened.

She gazed up at the Ferris wheel. She shuddered as she pictured herself plunging from the top.

"Please," he repeated. "I should have known this would happen. I told you, I haven't been at a carnival, since . . . you know . . . Judy's accident."

"Let's go back to the dorm," she said, turning away from the ride. "Maybe Holly's there."

"Okay," Chris agreed, reaching for her hand.

Tina quickly shoved her hands into her pockets. I can't lead him on anymore. From now on I'll be very cold, very careful.

She hurried through the throngs of people. A clown laughed too loud. Music blasted. Children screamed and ran around excitedly.

One more minute in this place and I'm going to explode! she thought.

Tina spotted the scooter. She jumped on. I want to look really good for Josh when he gets back, she thought as Chris started up the engine. I'll take a long bath and wash my hair and . . . Where is he taking me?

"Hey, Chris." She tapped him hard on the shoulder. "Isn't the dorm the other way?"

"I thought we'd go to my studio now. Take

some more shots for your portfolio!" he yelled back to her.

"Not now!" Tina protested. She tugged on his shirt sleeve. "Turn around."

Chris pulled over to the side of the road.

"It's only three," he explained. "Carla won't be back with the guys until at least five. This will be the only time to take some indoor shots."

"But I look awful," Tina argued, raking her hands through her tangled hair.

"No, you don't. Besides I have clothes there and makeup. Everything you need."

What if Chris freaks out again? she thought.

"Please. I told my uncle I'd be taking shots of you. He made me promise to show him the proofs."

This is my chance, Tina thought. If Rob Roberts likes the pictures, he could invite me to model for him!

She would have to keep a watchful eye on Chris. If he did anything weird, she would leave.

"Okay," Tina agreed. "But only for an hour."

"It's a deal." He held out his right hand.

Tina hesitated. Now I'm being silly, she thought. He just wants to shake hands.

Reluctantly she held out her hand. Chris gave it a quick shake.

They wove back into the traffic. Maybe I overreacted on the Ferris wheel, she thought.

Didn't Josh try something dumb like that once at a Fear Street Carnival? He and Jack Cooper tried to spin a race car off the track.

I don't think Chris meant to hurt me.

And he's going to show my photos to his uncle.

So at least something positive can come out of this horrible weekend.

They turned into a busy intersection. Tina glimpsed a girl kissing a guy near a parked car.

A girl with short dark hair. Wearing a white T-shirt with the words PATTERSON MAVERICKS on the back.

Tina squinted to get a better view.

Carla!

Carla didn't go to get the guys. She didn't leave the campus.

What is going on?

chapter

12

"**S**top! Chris—stop!" she screamed, tugging on his shoulders.

Chris slowed down and pulled over to the curb.

"We passed Carla!" Tina shrieked. "Kissing some guy!" She pointed down the block.

"Whoa!" Chris cried. "That's impossible."

"Go back!" Tina insisted. "Hurry!"

"It's a one-way street," he explained. "I'll have to circle the block."

"Hurry!" Tina urged. She wrapped her arms around Chris as he lurched back into the traffic.

What is happening? Tina wondered. Why did Carla lie to us?

Hurry! Hurry! she urged Chris silently. I have to confront Carla. I have to find out the truth!

But as Chris started a left turn, the scooter stalled.

"Nooo!" Tina wailed.

"I don't know what's wrong," Chris apologized. "Hang on. Keep your feet on the pegs."

He tried to turn the engine over. Nothing happened.

Cars rumbled by.

"What's wrong?" she demanded.

"I don't know," he replied. "Get off."

He pushed the scooter to the side of the road and studied the engine.

I could run back to where I saw Carla, Tina thought. But all the one-way streets are so confusing.

Chris tried the engine again and again. "Think I flooded it," he muttered.

"Let's run!" she pleaded.

"Here it comes," Chris said. "I feel it."

The engine coughed, then finally turned over.

"Hop on!" he cried.

Once again they cruised down the street. Chris made one left turn after another.

Where's he going? she thought. He's driving too far back.

"This street!" she yelled in his ear. "Turn here."

"Where?"

Tina searched the parked cars. "Over there! By that van!"

Chris pulled beside the van. No one there.

"I know it was Carla," Tina insisted as she climbed off the scooter. "Why is she still here?"

"She's not," Chris told her. "She can't be. She took my Jeep."

"But she was acting weird. Maybe she never left."

"Why would she lie?" Chris demanded.

Tina swallowed hard. Someone was lying. It had to be Carla.

"I don't think she left because for some reason she doesn't want me to see Josh," Tina blurted out.

"Carla and Steve have a date for the dance tonight," Chris reminded her. "She wants the guys back as much as you do."

As they argued, two girls passed on the opposite side of the street.

"Look at them," Chris said, pointing. "At the short one."

The girl wore jeans and a white shirt with the words PATTERSON MAVERICKS on the front and back. From a distance she could easily be mistaken for Carla.

"Okay. You got me," Tina admitted.

"Feel better?" Chris asked.

"Sort of," Tina lied. She didn't feel any better at all.

Every girl on campus could be wearing the same thing. The girl Tina saw was Carla. No doubt in her mind.

"We'd better get going," Chris urged. "We don't have much time left."

A few minutes later they turned onto a narrow, bumpy road. Tina held on tightly to Chris.

He slowed down in front of a large apartment building between two empty lots.

Vines snaked up the walls, covering most of the brick and framing the windows.

Chris pulled up the driveway. He revved the engine once before killing it. Then he hopped off.

"The studio is in the basement," Chris told her. He led her down a stairwell on one side of the building.

At the bottom of the stairs he unlocked a door that opened onto a long hallway. It smelled mildewy. A single bulb cast a dim light onto the dirty carpet.

"How did you ever find this place?" Tina asked.

"It took me a while," Chris replied. He strode to the door at the far end of the hall. "I wanted someplace quiet. Since it's in the basement, there's hardly any noise from the outside. It's perfect."

Chris unlocked the dead bolt and the two locks beneath it.

Why does he have so many locks? Tina wondered. I bet no one even knows this place is here.

"I have a lot of really expensive equipment inside," he explained, as if reading her thoughts. "You can never be too careful."

He swung open the door and stepped aside to let Tina in first.

As she entered the room, he flipped a switch. The lights flashed on, along with a song by the Psycho Surfers.

"I have the whole place wired through this switch," he explained, hanging his keys on a nail by the door. "I know the music is loud, but it helps me get in the right mood to work."

Tina's pulse raced with excitement. Everything in the room called for her attention. She didn't know what to study first.

The only outside light flowed through two small windows at ground level.

Soft beige carpeting covered the floor. Photographs and posters of models in gorgeous clothes lined the walls.

Wow! Tina thought. I recognize some of these

models. These photos must have been taken by his uncle.

But the shots of the unknown girls were equally striking. *I wonder if my pictures will turn out this good.*

"Look around," Chris said proudly. "I have to check on something in the darkroom."

He disappeared through a door on the far side of the room.

Tina walked around slowly, in awe of everything.

A long table with all kinds of props ran along one wall. A tripod, a tall fan, and a spotlight stood next to the table.

On a shelf stood several cameras, lenses, and dozens of film canisters.

In the far corner she spotted his desk. And next to that a stereo and a TV.

This is an awesome studio, she thought.

Excited, she wandered back along the wall, studying the photographs more carefully. She came to a display of girls in evening gowns. Each girl had signed her picture. The names Gabrielle, Francesca, and Tahnee jumped out at her.

She mumbled her own name. "Tina." *How boring. I'll have to change that.*

Next she came to a section of unusual photos. Lots of special effects.

"I thought I'd do one like this of you," Chris offered, putting his hands on her shoulders.

Startled, Tina turned around.

"How do you do that?" she asked.

She pointed to a photo of a girl sitting on the sand. The girl had deep red lips and nails. A blue shovel rose out of the sand next to her toe. The rest of the picture was in black and white.

"I color the black-and-white photos with these special pencils," Chris explained. "To get the effects I want. I could give you brown hair and green eyes."

"Well, you're the photographer. You can do whatever you want with me," Tina said.

Chris widened his eyes. "Whatever I want?"

Tina felt herself blush. "You know what I mean."

I shouldn't have said that, she scolded herself. I have to be careful. I can't lead him on again.

She turned back to the wall. Her eyes landed on a photo of a dark-haired girl with green eyes.

A chill crept down her spine.

Who's that? she thought. She looks like me. We could almost be twins, except for the hair and eye color.

The girl smiled at the photographer, her mouth half open, ready to speak. I can almost hear her voice, Tina thought.

What is she trying to tell me?

It gave her a shiver. She forced herself to turn away and continue down the wall.

Chris stayed close by her side.

She came to a photo of a sailboat. Its yellow and orange sail billowed in the wind. "Is this your boat?" Tina asked.

Chris didn't answer. He gazed at her, a solemn expression on his face.

I did it again, she thought. Why can't I remember to keep my mouth shut? He's thinking about Judy.

His eyes skimmed over her face and then drifted past her shoulder. He's reliving the accident, she thought.

The same way he did on the Ferris wheel.

Tina held her breath. Don't freak out again, Chris. Please.

Chris pulled his glasses out of his pocket and put them on. Then he ran his fingers through his hair.

"It *was* my boat," he replied bitterly, staring at the photograph.

A heavy silence fell over them. Tina pretended to study another photograph on the wall.

"There's makeup in the bathroom," Chris said softly. "Go put some on. You know, a lot of eye shadow and lipstick. And then we'll pick an outfit."

Chris turned away and busied himself choosing the correct lens and camera.

Tina made her way across the room. I wonder which is the bathroom, she thought. She knew the far door led into the darkroom. Two other doors stood side by side.

Tina chose the left one.

She reached for the doorknob.

"Don't open that!" Chris screamed.

Tina jerked her hand away.

Why did Chris sound so angry? she wondered.

He hurried up to her. "I'm sorry," he apologized. "There are a lot of chemicals in there that can't be exposed to the light."

Tina relaxed. "I thought it was the bathroom," she said. "I guess it's the next room, huh?"

Chris nodded. "I should have told you. It's my fault."

Tina opened the door and flipped on the light. Nothing happened.

"Oh, I forgot," Chris called in. "Use the switch by the mirror."

Tina slowly made her way through the dark bathroom, stretching her arms out in front of her. It's so dark in here, she thought. I can't see anything.

Her foot hit something hard. What's that?

Tina knelt down and ran her fingers across the floor.

Then she felt hair. Human hair.

Someone lay on the bathroom floor.

Still. So still.

Still as death.

chapter

13

"Chris!" she screamed. "Chris—help!"

She heard his hurried footsteps.

He plunged into the darkened room. She heard him click on the light.

She blinked. Stared down in horror at the body sprawled on the floor.

The mannequin body.

A mannequin wearing a red dress and a brown wig. The painted lips curved into a smile. The blue eyes stared blankly up at Tina.

"Oh! I—I'm sorry!" Tina stammered. "I thought—"

"That's Mary," Chris explained. "I use her to

test my lighting. I shouldn't have left her in here. Are you okay?"

"Yes. Fine." Tina struggled to slow her beating heart. "I'll get ready now."

Tina peered at herself in the mirror. The bright vanity lights revealed every pore on her face.

I have dark circles under my eyes, she thought.

She'd read about putting on makeup for a photo session in the fashion magazines. But this was her first real shoot.

She studied the makeup lining the counter. Chris had everything. Lipsticks of every color. Bright red. Deep brown. Magenta. White. Eyeliners and eye shadows. Creams and pencils and powders. I could stay in here all day, Tina thought.

"Start with the foundation," Chris instructed. He held his hand up to her face. "Ummm. Medium light."

Tina poured the liquid onto her hand and rubbed it into her face. Normally Tina wore very little makeup, but today was different. She applied charcoal-gray eyeliner on the top lid and the bottom. Then she added taupe shadow and lots of black mascara. She highlighted her cheekbones with a light coral blush and then put on a bright red lipstick.

She felt Chris watching her every move.

"More lipstick," Chris suggested. "And then

use this." He handed her a thin lip-liner brush. "Use a darker color to outline your lips."

"How's that?" She turned and smiled at him.

"You need to powder your face so it won't be shiny under the lights." He opened a drawer and removed a round container. Then he approached her with the powder. "I'll do it," he said.

This feels really weird, she thought as Chris dabbed her face. His eyes burned into hers as he worked, but she felt as though he were no longer looking at her, Tina Rivers. He was looking at her as if she were his creation.

From her fashion magazines she knew that Rob Roberts pampered his models during the photo shoots. He acted like their best friend. Then, after a big job was finished, he spent weeks on his yacht without talking to anyone. Only his cats.

Weirdness must run in the family, Tina told herself.

"Perfect," Chris said, stepping back. "Brush out your hair and let it hang loose. In the closet behind you are some outfits. Why don't we start with the red miniskirt and white crop top? And put on the red heels, okay?"

"Whatever you say," Tina replied.

"See you in a minute." Chris strode quickly from the bathroom.

Tina slid open the closet door. Along with the outfit Chris suggested, she saw several bodysuits, hip-hugger jeans, a gorgeous silk blouse. And half a dozen expensive-looking evening gowns.

Wow! she thought. Where did he get all these great clothes?

These are exactly what I'd buy at Dalby's in Shadyside. If I could afford to shop there.

She flipped through the dresses. Size six. Size six. Size six. Her size.

Helps to have money, she thought. Chris must go out and buy outfits for all his models.

She changed quickly. A full-length mirror hung on the back of the door. She twirled around in front of it.

I can't believe how perfectly everything fits, she thought. Josh would love me in this outfit. Maybe I can buy it from Chris.

The music changed to something she'd never heard before. She wondered what group it was.

"Ready?" Chris called out over the pounding music.

Tina opened the door. Chris stood at the camera, a serious expression on his face. He wore his glasses again.

"Where do you want me?" she asked shyly.

"Sit in the love seat and turn your head away from the fan."

Tina did as he said. The fan blew her hair. The bright light felt hot on her face.

Chris began clicking the shutter. Over and over.

"Give me a dreamy look," Chris said briskly. He pulled the camera off the tripod and moved closer to Tina. He lowered himself to his knees. "Cross your legs. Now look pouty."

His expression intense, he moved closer.

He's really into this, she thought. I hope I'm doing a good job.

"Put your fingers to your lips," he ordered. "As if you're trying to remember something."

He clicked the shutter several more times.

"Give me an *angry* expression." Chris emphasized the word *angry.*

That's easy, Tina thought. She pictured Carla. She bit down on her lower lip. Carla better be on her way to pick up the guys.

"Now show me you're in love," Chris demanded. He gazed at her through the lens.

Tina thought of Josh. Of his warm smile and thick, wavy hair. And his silly jokes that always cracked her up.

"Didn't you hear me?" Chris persisted. "I said you're in love. Give me more . . . more feeling. More!"

"I'm trying," she murmured.

Sweat trickled down Tina's face. Her hair blew into her eye. She wanted to scratch her cheek. But she knew she couldn't.

"No good." Chris sighed, setting the camera down. "You're starting to sweat."

He strode toward the bathroom and came back with the powder and two sodas. "Here." He sat down next to her on the love seat.

She took a swallow of the soda, then reached for the powder.

"I'll do it." Chris dabbed the powder on her forehead and cheeks. His hand lingered a second too long.

This is creepy, she thought.

She felt his eyes burn into hers. He leaned closer.

Tina glanced away. Please don't try to kiss me.

"I guess I need to get used to these lights," she said. I'll keep the conversation on photography, she decided. Keep it businesslike and friendly.

"No problem," he replied. "You're the best model I've worked with in a long time."

"Chris," Tina began. She stood up and smoothed out her skirt. "I just love this outfit. If you don't need it for another model, I'll buy it from you."

Chris remained silent.

"Or tell me where you bought it, and I'll see if they have another one," she suggested.

The faraway expression returned to his face.

What did I say? Tina's heart hammered against her chest. I said something wrong. I can feel it.

Chris stared at her.

What did I say?

"They were Judy's," he finally answered in a low, flat voice.

Judy's clothes!

A shiver ran down Tina's spine. I'm wearing a dead girl's clothes!

When she started to move away, he grabbed her hand. "Where do you think you're going?" he demanded. "We're not done yet."

"I . . . I wanted to change into something else. Maybe one of those dresses," she said shrilly.

"They're *all* Judy's clothes," Chris told her. "You're exactly the same size."

He saved all her clothes? Why? Every one of his models couldn't be a size six!

Tina felt too stunned to move.

"Go on," he commanded. "Get back on the love seat."

Tina's skin itched beneath the clothes. A dead girl had once worn this outfit. Did she ever go dancing in this skirt? Or to the movies? Did she go out with Chris in this outfit?

"Sit down and cross your legs," Chris instructed coldly.

Tina did as he ordered.

"No. The other way."

She couldn't seem to get the pose right. I can't concentrate, she thought. I have to get out of this skirt.

"I know what's wrong," Chris said.

He rushed into the bathroom and came back with the wig from the mannequin. "Here, put this on."

Tina stuffed her hair under the wig. Her scalp tickled. The hair fell to her shoulders in soft curls.

"Much better," he murmured.

He held the camera to his eye but didn't click the shutter. He kept focusing on her. He twisted the lens in and out.

Something's wrong, Tina realized. Why isn't he taking any pictures?

He moved closer and sat on the floor in front of her.

"I don't know why you dyed your hair blond in the first place," he scolded.

Huh? What did he say?

Tina toyed with the ends of the wig, keeping her gaze off Chris. Maybe if I don't make eye contact or say anything, he'll leave me alone.

"Judy," he snapped. "Look at me."

Judy? Did he call me Judy?

Tina stared into his eyes. And tried to remain calm.

"What's wrong with you today?" Chris asked. He sat down on the love seat.

Tina tucked her hands under her thighs. I won't let him touch me.

But Chris had his own ideas. He draped his arm around her and lowered his face inches from hers.

Tina pushed him away.

"What's the matter with you?" he asked. "You're the one who wanted me to take these shots. Don't I get anything in return?"

"Chris," Tina pleaded. "Please—"

"How about a kiss, Judy?" he demanded, lowering his face to hers. "How about a kiss? It's so nice to have you back."

chapter

14

Tina pushed him away and leaped to her feet.

He's crazy, she realized. I have to get out of here. Now.

Chris jumped up and moved toward her.

Get a grip, she told herself. He thinks I'm Judy. He loved Judy. He wouldn't hurt Judy. He won't hurt me.

She took a deep breath

He wants to kiss Judy. He doesn't really want to kiss me. All he's thinking about is Judy.

"Chris," she said calmly. "It's me, Tina. Remember? Josh's girlfriend."

He stared at her but didn't reply.

"Remember? I came up for the weekend, but Josh is delayed on a camping trip. Remember Carla is on her way to get Steve and Josh?" Tina continued. *Please remember.*

Chris turned his face away. When he turned back, his expression had changed. "You just look so much like . . . her. . . ." His voice trailed off.

"You shouldn't have made me put this wig on. And these clothes," she murmured.

"You're right," he agreed in a whisper.

"Chris, I know what happened was terrible. Losing Judy the way you did . . . It's horrible. Really horrible. But you have to believe me— you'll meet someone else one day," Tina told him. "You'll see. You'll get over your hurt. You'll find someone to make you happy. Someone to take away the pain."

Chris frowned. "Maybe."

Tina stood up. *I have to get out of these clothes,* she thought. *I have to get away from him.*

"Well, I think I've had enough modeling for today. I'm really tired. I guess I never realized how difficult posing is. So, I'll go change. Then I'm going back to the dorm." Tina started for the bathroom.

He grabbed her arm. "You're a great model," he said. "My uncle is going to be impressed with these shots."

Tina glanced down at his hand.

"Good," she answered. She didn't care if Rob Roberts ever saw the photos. She just wanted to get out of there.

"A few more shots," Chris insisted, holding on to her arm.

"No—" she started. "I'm really tired, and the lights made me feel a little queasy. I think I'm done."

She saw his eyes flare. She felt his hand tighten on her arm. He was getting that weird, dangerous look again.

I'd better play along, she decided. I'd better play along until I can get out of here safely. I can't afford to make him really angry.

"Well, okay," she agreed. "But let me go put my own clothes back on. I don't feel right in these clothes, you know what I mean?"

"Wait! I have a better idea." He pulled her toward the bathroom.

Tina's throat went dry. Now what?

From the back of the bathroom closet he pulled out an old-fashioned dress. Long and heavy, made from a deep blue fabric.

"It's from the eighteen-nineties," he explained. "My great-grandmother used to wear this."

"It's beautiful!" Tina exclaimed, a little relieved. This dress *definitely* did not belong to Judy.

"There's a bonnet on the prop table next to the cactus. Put that on," Chris instructed. "And touch up your lipstick. Make it a deep red. Okay?"

Tina nodded as Chris left the bathroom.

"Oh, and one more thing," he added, peeking his head back in. "Thanks for letting me take all these photos. They'll be great for my portfolio." He flashed her a big smile.

Tina forced herself to smile back at him. He looked perfectly normal again. In a way that made the whole situation even scarier. He switched back and forth between the sweet Chris, who was easy to talk to and lots of fun, to the intense, angry, creepy Chris. Which Chris would she have to deal with next?

Tina put her own clothes on under the old dress. Her plan was to get out of there just as fast as she could. Having her clothes on made her feel safer somehow.

The dress fit snug around the waist and then billowed out to the floor. With her clothes underneath, it was a little too tight.

First chance, I'll get out, she told herself. But I have to play along with him until I can get away.

She took a deep breath. The old dress cut into her waist.

Think positive. Stay calm.

Her fingers fumbled with the buttons of the dress. A heavy feeling knotted her stomach.

She searched the countertop for the dark red lipstick. She picked up tube after tube. Everything but dark red. It must be in one of the drawers.

She opened the top one. Two tubes of lipstick rolled around inside.

Reaching for one of them, she noticed an upside-down photograph. Curious, she picked it up and turned it over. Her breath caught in her throat. The hair on her arms stood on end. She looked at the photograph, turning it over again and again.

"I don't believe it!" she whispered.

chapter
15

Tina's hand trembled. She nearly dropped the photograph.

A photograph of herself.

Sleeping in her T-shirt in Josh's dorm bed.

The picture was taken last night.

Tina covered her mouth with her hand.

I can't scream. I have to stay calm.

But how can I stay calm?

Someone *had* been in her room.

Chris.

Chris had sneaked in and taken pictures of her while she slept!

He's really crazy, she realized.

He's crazy—and he might be dangerous.

What does he think? Does he think he can bring Judy back?

Does he think I'm Judy?

Tina reached under the dress and tucked the picture into her pocket. Her mind whirled quickly through her options.

She had only one. To get out. To get away from him. She peeked out of the bathroom. Chris tossed sand around on the floor and hauled a tall palm next to a beach blanket. Tina's throat tightened.

She glanced back at the hairless mannequin. The wide blue eyes and frozen smile made Tina shudder.

"What's taking so long?" Chris called out. "We're running out of time."

He's annoyed. I need to be careful.

"One minute," she called. "I'm putting my sneakers back on."

"Go barefoot. You're supposed to be at the beach!" he shouted.

When she came out, Chris was leaning over his desk, flipping through a magazine. "Look at these," he said. "I thought we'd do some like this."

Tina glanced at a photograph taken at a beach. Girls in long, colorful evening gowns smiled as they held fancy bottles of perfume.

"Sit down over there." He pointed to the

beach scene he had put together. Sand covered the ground. A blue backdrop for the sky. A beach ball rested on the floor.

Why an ocean scene? she asked herself. Judy died at the ocean. If I pose there, he'll think I'm Judy for sure.

She needed to distract him. Then she could run out of the studio.

"Lie down. I'll get a great shot of the sand running through your fingers," he suggested.

"It's not easy to lie down in this dress, but I'll try," she replied. "Just give me some time to figure out how to manage this skirt." She had to stall. No way did she want him to take these photos!

I have to get out of here, she told herself, thinking hard. He brought me a soda when he went to get the powder. I didn't see a cooler or anything in the bathroom. He must keep the sodas in the darkroom.

If I can get him to go to the darkroom, I can run out.

"Before we start," she asked, "could I have something to drink? It's so hot under these lights."

"Sure," he answered. "Anything for my top model."

Your *only* model, Tina thought bitterly. And soon you won't have any at all.

On the way to the darkroom Chris stopped.

Tina saw a cooler on the shelf beside the lenses.

Does he keep soda in there? If so, he won't have to go in the darkroom. How will I get out of here?

He opened the cooler and pulled out a bottle of developer. "The fridge is too small to keep some of the supplies in," he explained.

Good! The sodas weren't in that cooler.

A few more seconds, she told herself. Then run.

He walked slowly to the darkroom. She watched him open the door and disappear inside.

Now! Tina thought.

Lifting the old skirt, she plunged toward the exit.

Locked.

Why does he have all these locks? she thought, frantically fumbling with the top lock.

Turn to the left? No.

The right? Come on! Open up! Please!

Turn right? It must be to the right.

Open up, she pleaded. Open! Open!

The dead bolt snapped back. "Yes!"

She turned the knob again. The door didn't open.

Her heart pounded. Her hands shook.

"Be right out!" Chris yelled from the darkroom. "I'm checking on something."

One of the locks was still locked.

But which one? Which one?

She turned one. Then another.

Finally she pushed the door open.

I can't run in this dress, she realized.

Tina rushed into the gloomy hallway.

I have to get it off. She unbuttoned it as she ran.

Down the hall.

"Oh!" she cried out as a sharp pain jabbed her bare foot.

A jagged shard of glass.

Bending, she yanked it free. Blood flowed onto the dirty carpet.

Her foot hurt a lot, but she knew she had to keep going.

Don't stop, she told herself. No time now. Just get out.

Gasping for breath, she hobbled to the outer door. Only a few feet.

Her hands gripped the doorknob.

Locked! The outer door was locked, too!

The keys. Where were the keys?

Back in Chris's studio.

I'll go back inside, she decided. I'll pretend this didn't happen. Chris must still be in the darkroom.

She turned back, desperate to get the keys and get out of here.

She turned toward the studio—and bumped into Chris.

His face was twisted in a furious scowl.

"Where do you think you're going, Judy?" he demanded.

"Chris—I—I . . ." Tina sputtered. "Really, Chris. I have to go. This modeling just isn't for me. It's not your fault, but I just feel so self-conscious. And the lights . . . I—I . . . can't take the lights. . . . Please, Chris . . . Let me go!"

"Come back, Judy," he snarled. "Come back. I don't want to have to kill you again!"

chapter
16

*H*uh? Kill me? Tina thought, gripped with horror.

Wasn't Judy's death an accident?

Panic seized her chest. A cold sweat drenched her body. "Let go of me!" she cried.

Chris ignored her plea. He twisted her arm.

She stared into his eyes. Hatred. More hatred than she had ever seen in anyone's face.

Chris pushed her down the hallway. Back into the studio.

"Please—" she cried. "Please, Chris!"

No one knows where I am, she thought. No one.

Chris backed her toward the prop table. He gave her a hard shove. Her back hit the sharp thorns of the cactus. She heard the dress rip. The thorns pressed into her skin. "Did I hurt you?" he cried, breathing noisily.

Tina bit down on her lip.

"That's a good expression," he told her, his eyes wild. "I like it. Keep it. Let me get a shot."

Good. Go for your camera, she thought. Then I can make another run for it.

But he didn't look for a camera. Instead he made a circle with his fingers and raised it to his eyes. He stared at her through the pretend lens, pretending to focus.

"We made such a good couple. Why did you have to ruin everything?" he demanded. "Why? Answer me, Judy!"

He spun her around. Then he yanked her arm behind her back. He brought his other arm around her neck.

Tina could barely breathe. What was he going to do next?

"Come on, Judy," Chris rasped. "Don't fight it this time."

Tina kicked him in the leg. She swung her head back, bumping him in the teeth.

He laughed.

She smashed her bare foot against his ankle.

He laughed again. Such crazy, cruel laughter.

"Let me go!" she shrieked. "I'm not Judy!"

But she knew he wasn't listening now.

He wrapped his arm tighter around her neck. She sank her teeth into his skin.

"Oww!" he cried out. He loosened his grip.

With a desperate cry she wrenched herself free.

But he tackled her and threw her down on the floor. Her cheek slammed into the carpet. Pain shot down her body.

She tried to crawl away. But he grabbed her by the ankles and started to drag her across the floor.

Tina clawed at the carpet. But she couldn't free herself.

"Chris, please," she begged. "Let me go. Why are you doing this?"

"No more doing things your way, Judy," he growled.

"But I'm not Judy. Please!" she sobbed. "I'm Tina. *Tina.*"

"This time it's going to be the way I want it."

Chris pulled her into the darkroom.

"Have fun!" he shouted. He slammed the door hard. She heard the lock click.

Blackness surrounded her.

The air smelled sour. A bitter taste rose in her mouth. Chemicals, she thought.

With trembling hands she ripped off the old dress and tossed it into the darkness.

Her muscles ached. Her cut foot throbbed.

I need to stay calm, she thought. I need to think clearly. It's the only way to survive against a crazy person.

Slowly her eyes adjusted to the darkness. Objects in the room took shape.

A film enlarger. A paper cutter. The sink. A long table with trays of chemicals. A metal cabinet. Above her head, film negatives hung from nylon lines.

She found some paper towels and tape and fixed up a makeshift bandage for her bleeding foot. She wanted to be ready to run.

I have to find something to defend myself with, she thought. When Chris comes back, I have to be ready.

But will Chris return? she wondered.

Maybe Josh will come here and find me.

Yes.

I'll stay here until Josh comes and finds me. He'll be back soon. When I'm not at the dorm, he'll try here.

I'll stay inside the darkroom until help arrives. The nice, safe darkroom.

She could hear Chris ranting, on the other side of the door. "Not this time, Judy. This time I'm the boss."

The room began to spin. She felt as if she were back on the Ferris wheel, with the ground far below.

I'm thinking like a crazy person, she scolded herself. I can't stay in here. Safe? Who am I kidding?

I'll go insane, she thought. These walls will close in on me.

And any minute now Chris will come barging in. I need a weapon.

She spotted the overhead light. Standing up, she stretched her arm and clicked the light on. Red light washed over the room.

"No!" Tina shrieked. "Oh no!"

She wished she had never turned on the light.

chapter

17

Squinting through the red light, Tina's eyes swept over the walls.

Photos covered every inch.

Photos of her.

Large blowups of her eyes. Her lips.

Chris used the pictures I sent to Josh, Tina realized. Then he enlarged them and cropped them. She recognized bits and pieces of her life.

Her life. Her memories—on a crazy man's walls.

All here. Every one of them.

The photo taken at Christmas, sitting on her snowy front porch. A shot of Tina riding Buttercup, the mare at her uncle's farm in Georgia. One that Josh took of her in a bikini at his senior picnic at Fear Lake. And the prom picture.

Tina pulled it down and turned it over. The message she wrote to Josh covered the back. But Chris had changed Josh's name to his own.

Please Josh—find me! she thought desperately.

Shivers rolled down her body.

She hugged herself, rocking back and forth as she studied the photographs.

I can't believe this.

And then she found the creepiest one of all.

At the train station! A shot of her frightened face as she struggled with the man who tried to rob her.

Chris took her picture *before* he rescued her! Sick.

Is he taking pictures of me right now? she wondered. Maybe he has a peephole in the wall.

Is he watching me right now?

He's obsessed with me.

He was obsessed with Judy.

He killed Judy.

And I kissed him, Tina thought. He's a murderer and I kissed him. She cringed at the memory of Chris's hands gently moving down the side of her face.

If only she could disappear into one of those photos. Go back to a time when she felt safe.

"Josh—where are you?" she murmured. "Please hurry. Please!"

Her throat felt dry and scratchy. Tears collected in the corners of her eyes and then ran down her cheeks. I can't just sit in here and wait.

Wait to be murdered.

I have to pry the door open.

I have to get out of here.

Standing up, she glanced around for a sharp object. She needed something to stick in the lock.

Her eyes settled on the tall metal cabinet. Her legs trembled as she made her way across the darkroom.

Be strong, she told herself. Everything is going to be okay.

But the moment she pulled open the cabinet door, Tina knew that nothing would be okay again.

The rancid smell hit her first.

Her stomach tightened. A sour taste collected on her tongue.

"Nooo!" A low wail escaped her throat.

She forced her eyes up to the face. What remained of the face.

The sunken eyes staring blindly back at her. Solid like egg whites.

Those clothes.

She recognized the black T-shirt with the mountains on the front.

She bought that shirt. She remembered she bought it the day he got his acceptance at Patterson.

No. It's not him. It's not him. It's not.

Tina screamed.

Josh's stiff body tumbled to the floor.

chapter

18

Tina choked on her tears.

She forced herself to roll the corpse onto its back.

Josh's face . . . his handsome face . . .

The skin had been eaten away, exposing his nose and cheekbones.

The skin on his forehead flapped loose. Tina saw tiny red veins along his hairline.

Most of his beautiful thick brown hair had been burned away.

Chemicals? Had Chris used chemicals to kill Josh?

No. She noticed a deep gash on the side of his head. Chris must have surprised Josh by throwing the chemicals in his face. Then Chris smashed him over the head.

A cold shiver ran down her spine. She reached for his hand. So cold. Cold and stiff.

Tina felt the bile rise into her throat. She dropped the hand, turned her head away, and gagged.

She wondered what Josh's last thoughts had been. Did you think of me, Josh?

I love you. I love you so very much.

"Judy!" Chris's shout burst into her thoughts. He yanked open the door.

His eyes widened in shock. His mouth dropped open as he saw Tina kneeling beside Josh.

Doesn't he know what he did? Tina wondered with a sob. Doesn't he remember?

"Judy," he whispered, taking her hand. He pulled her to her feet. Smiling, he took her face in his hands.

His skin felt rough as he ran his fingers along her cheekbone.

He's a murderer, Tina thought. And he's touching me. So gently. I can't stand it.

"Nothing can ever keep us apart again. Nothing," he whispered. His eyes darted around the red room and then stared into hers.

Tina shivered. He's completely insane.

"I'm almost ready," he whispered. "We can leave in a few minutes."

"Leave?" Tina managed to choke out. "Where . . . where are you taking me?"

"Don't play dumb, Judy. You know how I hate that."

Tina knew she wasn't strong enough to fight him off. I'll try to and reason with him, she thought. It worked before. Maybe it will work again.

"We'll be fine together. You'll see, Judy." Chris swung her hand back and forth.

He's acting as though we're standing on the street somewhere, having a friendly conversation, she thought. Not in a darkroom, with Josh's dead body lying on the floor.

"Chris," Tina said, struggling not to burst out in loud sobs.

"Yes?" He squeezed her fingers tightly.

"You won't get away with this," she murmured. "People will start searching for me and . . ." She swallowed hard. "Josh. People will wonder where I am."

"No one will try to find you, Judy," He dropped her hand and began staring at the photos. "They don't send out a search party for someone who's already dead."

"They'll put you in jail, Chris. Do you want to

spend the rest of your life behind bars?" Tina demanded in a trembling voice.

"I'm spending the rest of my life with you, Judy." His eyes traveled over her. From her head to her toes and back to her face again.

I should have realized at the train station that he was obsessed with me, she thought. Why didn't I see it?

Chris grinned at her. So pleased with himself.

Stay calm, she instructed herself. Stay calm. It's the only way you'll get out alive.

"If you let me go now, I won't tell anyone, I promise," she lied.

Slowly she backed away from him.

"Where are you going?" he asked sharply.

"Nowhere."

"That's good, Judy." He moved closer. "I'm glad you finally realize that I'm right."

She inched back. "I do, Chris," she murmured. "I do."

Tina backed into the developing chemicals.

That's it, she thought. Now you're going to pay for what you did to Josh.

She grabbed the closest tray. Acid. This has to be the same acid he burned Josh with.

Chris smiled at her.

The smile was still on his face as she pulled back her arm—and heaved the acid into his face.

chapter

19

*T*he liquid splashed over Chris's face.

He uttered a startled cry—and rubbed his eyes.

But when he lowered his hands, his face revealed only anger, not pain.

"You picked the wrong tray, Judy," he rasped. "It was only water."

Water! Tina felt the floor crumble away beneath her.

"You never cared about my photography, did you?" he accused. He crossed the room quickly, water dripping down his cheeks.

He reached toward the other two trays.

Tina gasped.

What is he going to do? Tina wondered.

He glanced up at the photos on the wall. "Such a pretty face," he murmured.

With a sweep of one hand he sent the trays clattering to the floor. The liquid splashed into the air. Tina flinched.

The liquid splashed up.

Tina jumped back. But a drop of liquid spotted her arm.

She stared down in horror as a tiny circle of skin sizzled and then peeled away.

Is this what Josh's face felt like?

A horrified sob escaped her throat.

"Did you think I was going to throw it at you?" Chris demanded. He ran his finger down her cheek. "I wouldn't ruin a pretty face like this. Together we're going to get rich. You and me."

I have to get out of here before he kills me, Tina told herself.

She searched the darkroom frantically for something heavy. Something to throw at him. "You're already rich. You have everything."

"Everything?" he answered. He looped his arm through hers. *"Now* I have everything. All I ever wanted was you, Judy. I can't understand why you never realized that. But that's all in the past. Let's go."

He started to pull her out of the darkroom.

Tina spotted a metal tripod on the floor near the enlarger. Perfect.

This better work.

She glanced down at Josh's body sprawled on the floor.

Then she let out a horrified gasp.

"Chris! It's Josh! He's moving. He's getting up!"

chapter
20

"*H*uh?"

Chris spun around.

Tina picked up the tripod—and swung it hard.

It made a cracking sound as it hit Chris's face.

Blood trickled from his nose.

His eyes bulged in surprise.

As he raised his hands to his face, Tina swung the tripod again.

"I hate you!" she shrieked. "You killed Josh!"

She raised the metal into the air for a second time.

Chris started to turn away.

The tripod caught him on the back of the head. He groaned and slumped to the floor.

His body sprawled alongside Josh.

Sobbing, Tina let the tripod fall.

Cold sweat drenched her body. She wrapped her arms around herself.

Did I kill Chris? Did I?

As she gazed down at the two still bodies, nausea flooded her.

She leaned over the sink and vomited.

There's nothing left in me, she thought. Nothing at all.

She wiped her sweaty hands on a paper towel.

Gasping for air, Tina stumbled out of the darkroom.

The police, she thought. I have to call the police.

Her legs trembled. She could hardly make it to the phone.

Be strong, she told herself. Get help.

I have to turn the music off, she decided. I can feel it throbbing in my head. She stumbled to the sound system and fumbled with the buttons until the music stopped.

In the quiet Tina thought she heard a faint pounding noise. Behind her.

She spun around. "Chris?"

No. No one there.

Tina stared at the closet door. The door Chris wouldn't let her open.

What could be in there?

With small, cautious steps Tina approached the door.

Maybe I shouldn't open it, she thought.

She pressed her ear to the door.

You've got to open the door, she told herself. You have to find out what he didn't want you to see.

Fear clutched at her heart.

Open it! she ordered herself.

She rested her hand on the knob.

She pulled open the door.

"Holly!" Tina shrieked.

Her cousin lay dead on the floor.

chapter

21

Dead? No!

Holly's arms and legs were tied. Her brown hair fell over her face. She groaned.

"Hunnnh?" Holly raised her face, her eyes still shut.

She's alive!

Tina dropped to her knees beside her. "Holly? Holly? Are you okay? Are you alive? Holly? Please be okay, Holly. Please!"

Tears rolled down Tina's cheeks. She grabbed Holly in an emotional hug. "I can't believe I finally found you. It's been so awful. So awful."

Holly blinked several times. She shook her head, dazed. She finally opened her eyes. She squinted hard at Tina, trying to focus. "Tina—it's you! Oh, wow . . . How long have I been in this closet?"

"I—I don't know," Tina stammered.

"I was so scared. Chris kept yelling that I'd ruined his plans. He wanted you all to himself," Holly sobbed. "He tied me up and left me in here. In the dark. I didn't know how much time passed. I didn't know what he planned to do. I—I thought he was going to leave me in here forever!"

Tina struggled to untie her cousin's arms and legs. The thin cords scratched her fingers. Her hands shook so hard, it seemed to take forever.

"Hurry. Please hurry," Holly pleaded. "My whole body—it's asleep. I've got to move, Tina. I've got to get away from here. I've been so frightened. I thought I was going to die. I really did."

Holly was in the closet the whole time, Tina thought, fumbling with the tight cords. While I was posing for Chris, Holly was in the closet.

"Josh is dead!" Tina blurted out.

Holly uttered a sharp cry. "No, Tina. No. I'm so sorry."

Tina tugged frantically at the knotted cords.

"I—I think I killed Chris," Tina continued. "I hit him. Hard. In the back of the head."

Holly shook her head, still dazed. She seemed to be having trouble taking in all that Tina was telling her. "You hit Chris? With what?"

"With his tripod. I heard his skull crack. I—"

"You killed him?" Holly's voice came out hoarse, trembling.

"I think so," Tina told her. "I'm not sure. But I think I did."

The cord slid off Holly's ankles. She groaned, rubbing her legs. "I don't know if I can walk. I've been in here so long. Locked in the darkness. Since after the party."

"How did he get you up here?" Tina asked.

"Chris introduced me to a guy," Holly explained. "At the party. I went into town with him. We went to a club. It got really late."

"You didn't come back to the dorm?" Tina asked.

"Yes. I did," Holly replied. "Around four. But when I got to the room, Chris jumped out. I guess he was waiting for me. He grabbed me. He hit me over the head with something."

Holly rubbed her head. Tina saw a knot of clotted blood in her hair.

"I woke up in this closet," Holly told her. "I—I was so frightened, Tina."

"He's crazy," Tina murmured. "Chris is totally crazy. He thought I was Judy. His old girlfriend."

139

"I knew he was weird. From the minute I met him," Holly replied. She struggled unsteadily to her feet. "Come on. Let's get out of here."

Holding hands, they stumbled out of the closet.

"We're safe now," Tina told Holly.

But I won't feel safe, she thought, until I'm far from this studio.

She glanced over at the sand. Only half an hour ago Chris wanted her to pretend she was enjoying herself at the beach.

Pretending.

That was Chris's life. He pretended to be a nice guy. He pretended Judy was still alive.

Tina shuddered.

Still holding on to Holly, she started for the door.

"What—what's that?" Holly stammered. "Is someone else in here?"

Tina heard it, too. Footsteps.

Tina spun around.

Chris!

Chris! Alive!

He staggered from the darkroom, bright red blood streaming down his face.

He raised long, pointed scissors into the air.

"Good-bye, Judy," he choked out, swinging the scissors in front of him, snipping the blades in the air.

Snip. Snip. Snip.

"Good-bye, Judy." Blood dripped from his mouth and down his chin, as he rasped the words.

He moved with surprising quickness.

Tina tried to back away.

She stumbled.

Hit the wall.

Chris raised the scissors over her head.

The studio door burst open.

Carla and a tall blond-haired boy rushed in.

"Carla—help us!" Tina shrieked. "Carla—thank goodness you're here!"

Chris lowered the scissors. He turned to Carla. He breathed a sigh of relief. "What took you so long?" he demanded. "They almost got away."

chapter

22

"Carla—?" Tina gasped. "Carla—you're not on Chris's side—are you? Have you been helping Chris this whole time?"

"What took you so long?" Chris demanded sharply. He wiped blood off his chin with the back of his hand. He rubbed the back of his head—the spot where Tina had hit him—and groaned.

"Carla—?" Tina cried.

Carla brushed past Holly and Tina and made her way toward Chris. "Chris—the blood. Your head. Are you okay? You're totally cut."

"What happened here?" the blond boy demanded. "How did you get hurt? Should we get a doctor?"

"I'm okay, Steve," Chris replied softly. He gestured with the scissors. "Just a little trouble here. But it's all under control now that you and Carla are here. What took you so long?"

Tina felt so hurt, so furious, she thought she might explode. "Carla—how could you help him?" she shrieked. "How could you be so evil?"

Steve and Carla ignored her, acted as if she weren't in the room, acted as if she weren't holding on to her cousin, screaming at them.

"Hey, man, let me see your head," Steve said, moving toward Chris.

Chris raised the scissors menacingly. "Get back. I *told* you I'm okay."

Steve raised both hands. "Okay. Okay." He backed off quickly.

Carla turned and pointed to Tina and Holly. "What's with them?"

"He killed Josh!" Tina wailed. "He's a murderer! He killed Josh. How can you help him now? He's a murderer! Doesn't that mean anything to you?"

Carla continued to ignore Tina. She moved toward Chris. "I'm here to help you, Chris. You know that. You do know that—don't you?"

"We're both here to help you," Steve said. "What can we do?"

Chris rubbed the back of his head. He winced in pain. Tina could see him struggle to keep his eyes in focus. "Judy won't pose for me anymore," he told his friends. "I want to get a few more shots."

"Okay," Carla replied. "Steve and I will help. How about if I take a shot of you and Judy together? For your portfolio."

"No!" Tina cried. "You're *both* crazy! I'm *not* Judy, and I'm not posing with him!"

Carla shot her an angry look.

"Better do what she says," Holly whispered.

I can't sit next to him, Tina thought. I won't. I'd rather die than have him touch me again.

"Steve, bring me a camera," Carla instructed, keeping her eyes on Chris.

Steve walked over to the table, picked up a camera, and handed it to Carla.

"Here." Carla held it out to Chris. "You adjust the settings, and I'll take the picture."

She turned to Tina. "Judy, stand over here." She motioned Tina over toward Chris. "Hurry."

Tina swallowed. I can't. I can't.

"Take your camera," Carla urged Chris. She held it out to him.

Chris reached for the camera.

Carla grabbed the scissors from his hand.

"Grab him!" she shouted to Steve. "Quick!"

Steve dived forward.

Wrapped his arms around Chris.

Dragged him to the floor.

As Tina stared in shock, Chris slumped to the floor. He didn't struggle. He curled up, covering his face with his hands. "Why'd you have to ruin it again? Why?" he wailed. "Why?"

Carla hurried over to Tina and Holly. "I'm so sorry." Carla slid her arm around Tina. "I didn't know. I didn't know what he was doing. I can't believe he killed Josh. I really can't!"

"You—you didn't work with him?" Tina demanded. "You weren't helping him with the whole thing?"

"No!" Carla cried. "No. You've *got* to believe me! Steve and I played along with him now—just so we could get the scissors away from him, just so we could make sure you were safe."

Tina sighed. "I . . . believe you."

Holly wrapped Tina in a hug. The three girls clung to each other.

Steve stood guard over Chris, never shifting his gaze away.

Tina sobbed. "You should see Josh's face."

"I'm calling the police," Holly said.

"I feel so horrible," Carla murmured. "Chris told me Josh was with another girl this weekend. He said Josh had been secretly going out with her

145

for months. Oh, Tina, I'm so sorry. Chris said we had to keep you from finding out about the other girl."

"I was camping in the mountains," Steve said. "Carla told me Josh was off with some girl, and you were here with Chris."

"That's when Steve set me straight," Carla interrupted. "Steve told me that Chris was lying. He told me that Josh hasn't been with anyone but you. He said that Josh had been planning all week for your visit."

"That's why he didn't go on the camping trip," Steve explained.

Tina let the tears roll down her cheeks. Poor Josh.

"That's when I panicked," Carla told Tina. "Josh wasn't with another girl and he wasn't camping with Steve. So where was he? That's when I figured Chris had done something to him."

"He murdered Judy, too. He told me," Tina choked out. "I should have suspected something. I—I—"

"Oh, I should have figured it out. He'd go into these deep depressions over Judy," Steve broke in. "If you talked to him, he wouldn't even hear you. He talked about Judy all the time."

"The police will be here in a minute," Holly

announced, returning. "This weekend has been such a nightmare. Such a horrible nightmare."

Slumped on the floor, Chris raised his eyes to Tina. "I'll develop your pictures, Judy. Tomorrow. You'll like them. This time you'll really like them. You'll be so happy, Judy. I'll make you happy. I really will."

Tina covered her ears with her hands and rushed out of the studio. I can't listen to him anymore! she told herself. I can't!

She didn't stop running until she reached fresh air. Then she flung herself down on the grass and took several deep breaths.

The air filled her lungs. Her body relaxed. She heard sirens in the distance. Finally help was on its way.

Tina gazed into the darkening sky. Her eyes settled on the first star of the evening.

No wish tonight, she thought.

No wish at all.

Tina knew that no matter how hard she wished, she would never be able to erase this weekend from her memory.

About the Author

"Where do you get your ideas?"

That's the question that R. L. Stine is asked most often. "I don't know where my ideas come from," he says. "But I do know that I have a lot more scary stories in my mind that I can't wait to write."

So far, he has written over fifty mysteries and thrillers for young people, all of them bestsellers.

Bob grew up in Columbus, Ohio. Today he lives in an apartment near Central Park in New York City with his wife, Jane, and fourteen-year-old son, Matt.

THE NIGHTMARES
NEVER END . . .
WHEN YOU VISIT

Next, the first in a new trilogy . . .
THE CATALUNA CHRONICLES
BOOK #1: *THE EVIL MOON*
(Coming in August 1995)

They came from different worlds. Different times. But they were destined to meet.

1698, West Hampshire Colony

Catherine Hatchett longed to be accepted by the people of her colony. But they believed the red crescent-moon birthmark on her forehead brought them bad luck. They blamed Catherine for the crops that withered in the fields, and the animals that lay dying in the pastures.

And they came to hang her for sins she did not commit!

1995, Shadyside

Bryan Folger knew his rich girlfriend, Misty, looked down on him—even though she swore she didn't. If he could just buy the Cataluna, everything would be different. The sleek white car would impress Misty and all his friends. And Bryan would do anything to get it.

Steal . . . even kill!

What powerful, dark forces bring Bryan and Catherine together? Discover the terrible truth in *THE EVIL MOON*.